Claire's jaw ... **to speak and** ... **last an "Oh, m**... **mouth.**

"Awesome tree, isn't it?" Alex asked.

"You shouldn't have. You know how I feel about…this," she snapped.

It struck him how beautiful she was when she was angry. But then her shoulders slumped and moisture brimmed in her eyes, effectively dousing the fire he'd seen before. Anger he could handle, but not tears.

Remorse filled him and he stepped forward to wrap his arms around her. "I'm sorry. We only wanted to bring you a piece of Christmas. I didn't intend to push you so hard or upset you."

Clarie buried her face in his coat and nodded.

She'd taken several big steps to move on with her life, he thought, but until she worked through her aversion for this winter holiday her past would always have an unrelenting grip on her. Perhaps he wouldn't care about that state of affairs if he was only interested in an occasional evening with her. The fact was, he wanted to enjoy every season of the year with her, including Christmas.

Jessica Matthews's interest in medicine began at a young age, and she nourished it with medical stories and hospital-based television programmes. After a stint as a teenage candy-striper, she pursued a career as a clinical laboratory scientist. When not writing or on duty she fills her day with countless family and school-related activities. Jessica lives in the central United States with her husband, daughter and son.

Recent titles by the same author:

A WHITE KNIGHT IN ER
A MOTHER'S SPECIAL CARE
A DOCTOR'S HONOUR
A NURSE'S COURAGE

A VERY SPECIAL CHRISTMAS

BY
JESSICA MATTHEWS

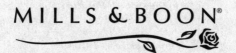

MILLS & BOON®

*First published in Great Britain 2003
Harlequin Mills & Boon Limited,
Eton House, 18-24 Paradise Road, Richmond, Surrey TW9 1SR*

© Jessica Matthews 2003

ISBN 0 263 83486 7

*Set in Times Roman 10½ on 11¼ pt.
03-1203-48421*

*Printed and bound in Spain
by Litografía Rosés, S.A., Barcelona*

CHAPTER ONE

"WHAT do you want first? The good news, or the bad?"

"Tough decision." Claire Westin peered over her freshly poured morning cup of coffee to smile up at the physician who'd hired her two months ago. "Which would you rather give?"

Alex Ridgeway shrugged shoulders that were too broad and too tempting to be ignored. At six-four, he towered over her by at least seven inches and the height difference made it effortlessly easy to gaze at the sexy hollow of his throat.

"I asked you first," he reminded her with a grin that made him appear twenty-five instead of ten years older.

Because their offices weren't officially open this early, he hadn't covered his street clothes with his usual white coat, so she could see the play of biceps under his tan sweater. His muscles and bone structure, not to mention skin that hadn't completely lost its summer tan, provided a prime reason to wish for hot weather when tank tops and shorts were in vogue. If he mowed his yard shirtless, she could sell tickets to women all over town. She'd make a small fortune, too, but she doubted if Alex would agree.

What a tragedy to let such eye candy go to waste!

His dark hair and well-defined features made him quite striking as far as looks were concerned, although the thin scar bisecting his right eyebrow was the only imperfection she could see. If she'd been brave enough to ask about it, she would have, but she'd decided that he'd probably earned it playing sports since he had the tall, lean body of a basketball player and large hands to match. Size notwithstanding, those long fingers were gentle enough to soothe a baby's cry, yet powerful enough to yank a dislocation into place.

But he was waiting for an answer, not an assessment of his appearance. "I'd rather not ruin my day right away, so give me the good news first," she said.

"Henry Grieg gave us a hundred dollars to spend."

Claire knew better than to look a gift horse in the mouth, but if the money was intended for medical equipment, it wouldn't buy much. "And that's cause for a celebration?"

"Yes and no."

She chuckled. "Which is it? And why do I sense this is tied to the bad news?"

Alex grinned. "It's not really bad news. It's an assignment." Then, like a little boy who couldn't hold his secret any longer, he added, "You and I are in charge of decorating the Christmas tree in our group's waiting room."

To Claire, this was Bad news, with a capital B. The last time she'd gotten caught up in the season had been three years ago, and it had turned into the worst holiday of her life. Since then, she'd done her best to ignore Christmas as much as anyone could who was surrounded by people who went overboard.

To hide her dismay, she sipped her coffee without thinking and instant fire filled her mouth. She squealed.

"What's wrong?" he asked, his dark brows drawn together in a straight line. "Too hot?"

She nodded. "Burned my tongue."

"Bummer."

"Yeah. But back to decorating. Why us? We're the new kids on the block."

Alex filled his mug, a ceramic cup that was emblazoned with WORLD'S GREATEST DAD and stirred in the ice he'd chipped out of the freezer tray. "Exactly."

"Ah. I get it now. No one else wants the job, so we're elected by default."

He grinned. "Not quite."

His jovial attitude was oddly suspicious. It was one thing for Dr Grieg to assign her to the task and another for Alex to speak for her. "Don't tell me you volunteered."

He raised his drink to his mouth, drawing her gaze to full lips and a square jaw. "He caught me as I was leaving last night and asked if we'd be willing."

She sank onto a chair, struggling to keep her voice even. "And you agreed."

"What else could I do?"

"Refuse," she said promptly.

"He may have asked ever so politely, but I caught the distinct impression that I didn't have a choice. We have to take our turn, you know."

Alex had moved to Pleasant Valley last summer, while she'd arrived six weeks ago, in the middle of October.

"That may be, but I'm surprised he doesn't want people who are more familiar with how the clinic as a whole handles the holiday." She hated the desperate sound in her voice, but it matched the way she felt.

"New blood brings new ideas, or so Henry believes."

This new blood was fresh out of ideas and didn't want to think of any. "I thought the doctors and their wives-slash-girlfriends were responsible for decorating."

"They are, but since I don't have either, I need you to stand in as my assistant. For the record, Henry mentioned you himself." Alex studied her with a gaze that was far more intent than she liked. "Is there a problem?"

Yes, she wanted to shout. There is. Instead, she hesitated. So much for hoping she could talk someone else into helping Alex, someone like her friend Nora Laslow, who'd encouraged her to apply for this job in the first place. Should she explain her feelings about Christmas? How this season was more depressing than enjoyable? And what good would it do? Alex was counting on her. Henry had issued his directive and, unless one had a sound reason against it, his word was law.

Of course, she could explain to Alex—he'd understand because that was the sort of man he was—but did she want to? She'd come to Pleasant Valley to start over, and holding back the nitty-gritty details of her history was part of it. She intended to move forward at a snail's pace, not at jet speed. But since she had no choice, she'd simply have to muddle through as best she could.

"No," she finally said. "I just wish you'd cleared this with me beforehand."

"I couldn't. You'd already left and, like I said, I didn't have much choice. If you're afraid of the amount of time it will take, don't," he assured her. "I talked it over with Jennie and she's willing to help us this afternoon."

"Then you shouldn't need me." Relief swept through her. His eight-year-old daughter could handle hanging ornaments and flinging tinsel over the tree.

He frowned, and for an instant she was afraid he'd ask questions about her blatantly obvious reluctance. "Actually, I do," he said. "First of all, each department holds a contest for everything from The Prettiest to The Most Unusual. According to Henry, we can choose any theme we'd like and we're not under any pressure to win anything. Although he did mention that our department has won one category or another for the last three years."

Themes? Prizes? This didn't sound at all like slapping a few ornaments on a tree and calling it good. This sounded like serious business.

It was also business that she didn't want to take on in any way, shape or form. She simply didn't have the heart for it.

"Any suggestions?" he asked.

"Sorry." Claire shook her head for emphasis. "You've thought about this longer than I have."

"How do you feel about snowflakes and icicles?"

Cold and ice. No one could have described how her heart felt during this time of year more perfectly.

"Sounds good to me." At least he hadn't proposed angels. She didn't think she could bear that. "Where are you going to find what we need on such short notice?"

"Last night we went to the store for ideas. We found glass icicles and Jennie volunteered to cut out snowflakes." He grinned. "She was so excited, she started on them as soon as we came home. She loves Christmas, you know."

"So I assumed."

Claire wondered if she'd ever see Joshua anticipate the season as eagerly as Jennie did, but to do that, she'd have to get caught up with holiday joy herself. For his sake, she should, but she had a few years before he'd question why they didn't observe Christmas like everyone else.

"Anyway," he continued, "now that we've agreed on a theme, we're going back to the store during our lunchbreak to buy the supplies. I'd hoped you'd ride along."

"I can't today," she said, trying to sound disappointed when she wasn't. "I may get my hair cut if my hairstylist can work me in."

Alex's gaze flitted over her hair, and she was tempted to run her hand over her short, straight locks. "Looks great to me."

She smiled. "Thanks, but, believe me, I need to visit my hairdresser. Don't worry. I'm sure whatever you buy will be fine. Just let me know how much I owe you."

"Nothing," he said. "Henry gave me a hundred dollars, remember?"

"Ah, yes. Our good news," she said dryly. "Will that be enough?"

He looked horrified. "I hope so. Even if it isn't, we can't spend a penny more. To keep things fair, we're required to work within a budget." He switched gears. "Can you think of anything else we might need? I'd hate to forget the obvious.''

"Snowflakes and icicles. I'd say you've covered the main elements," she said.

"Then it's settled." He rose. "Are you going to the staff meeting now?"

Claire would rather have skipped it, but Henry was a stickler for attendance. "Yes, but I have to make a quick phone call first."

"I'll see you there."

He left, and instantly Claire was aware of how empty a room seemed without him. He had a presence that always engulfed her, which was disconcerting to say the least. Oddly enough, he was the only man she'd been around since Ray's death who caused that sort of inexplicable reaction.

Although he was Available, with a capital A—happily divorced, according to Nora—he seemed more interested in raising his eight-year-old daughter, Jennie, than in pursuing a love life.

She felt the same way. Joshua demanded her attention and, being his only parent, she wanted to provide twice as much to compensate for her missing other half.

After she called the beauty shop and heard the news that she'd have to wait until Wednesday, she hurried to the conference room and ran into Nora.

Nora and Claire had been classmates at nursing school and their friendship had lasted for eleven years. She was a vivacious, petite blonde who worked for Dennis Rehman, the newlywed physician of the bunch. She was also on a perpetual diet to shed the thirty extra pounds her three pregnancies in five years had given her.

"Don't sit at the table," Nora told Claire as she steered her toward the chairs against the wall.

"Why not?"

"Because someone brought *crème*-filled donuts and my willpower this morning is at an all-time low."

"OK."

Fortunately for Nora, the seats around the conference table—and the donuts—were taken. Alex was sitting beside his three colleagues—Dennis Rehman, Mike Chudzik and Eric Halverson—while Henry Grieg stood at the front of the room. He tapped his fountain pen against his cup and the gathering quieted.

"I'll make this short and sweet, people," he said. "I'm sure you've received your notices from the hospital about delinquent charts. You also know how I feel about those, so if the letter applies to you, I suggest you do something about it."

One of the things that impressed Claire was Alex's attention to detail. He was the last person she'd ever expect to fall too far behind in his paperwork.

After discussing the status of this quarter's budget, Henry finished with, "This is a reminder that our group is responsible for the behind-the-scenes work for this year's clinic Christmas party."

"Has it been five years since the last time we were the hosts?" Mike Chudzik asked. Mid-fortyish, he was a short, balding fellow with a schoolteacher wife and two elementary school children.

Henry nodded. "Orthopedics was in charge last year and our turn in the rotation comes after theirs. As you can imagine, I'm expecting everyone to pitch in. Amy has the sign-up sheet and there are still plenty of open job slots.

"And don't think you can get by with not helping," he warned as he peered over his reading glasses to survey those squeezed into the conference room like sardines. "There are twenty slots and twenty staff members, so I'll know if someone doesn't volunteer. I'm expecting one hundred per cent participation."

Claire mentally groaned. With more than thirty physicians, who represented nearly every major medical specialty in the Pleasant Valley Clinic, and nearly three hundred support staff members, including Lab, Pharmacy, Radiology and Maintenance, she'd hoped no one would notice her absence. Fat chance. She hadn't counted on the family practice group playing a key role. It was just her luck that she had to partake in the festivities her first year here.

If only she'd applied for a job in Orthopedics...

Surely there would be some way she could wiggle out of whatever responsibility Henry might have for her. It was bad enough she'd gotten roped into decorating, but she drew the line at attending a party, in any capacity. If nothing else, her son Joshua was two, and everyone knew that illness struck two-year-olds at a moment's notice. She didn't want him sick, of course, but she was desperate enough to pretend that he was.

The rustle of people rising off their chairs signaled the end of the meeting. By virtue of their late arrival and the seats they'd taken, Claire and Nora were some of the last to leave the conference room. Claire took advantage of those few, relatively private moments to discuss the subject that had tied her in knots.

"Did you hear?" she asked in a tone meant for Nora's ears only. "I'm supposed to decorate the office Christmas tree with Alex."

Nora winked at her. "You lucky dog, you. I know of several nurses in Oncology who would love to be in your shoes."

"They can have them," Claire said fervently.

"No can do. The tree has to be decorated by people in the department or we'll be disqualified."

"Maybe Hattie will take my place." Hattie had come out of retirement to work as Eric's nurse while his regular assistant, Christina, was on maternity leave.

"You'll be fine."

"I can't do it. As for attending a party?" She shook her head. "It's out of the question."

"I know it will be tough—"

"Try impossible."

"Some things are," Nora agreed, "but this isn't."

Claire disagreed. "You have to think of someone who'll fill in for me."

"No."

"I'll beg if I have to."

"I don't want you to beg. I want you to reconsider."

"Why?"

"You moved here to start over, which was long overdue, if you ask me."

Nora had suggested a change eighteen months ago, but it had taken a while for Claire to consider the idea, then to make plans and finally to implement them. "I'll admit I didn't rush into uprooting Joshua and me, but we're here and we're adjusting."

"So adjust a little more."

"Easy for you to say."

"You'd be finished if you'd been working instead of whining," Nora pointed out.

Nora was right—Claire *had* spent a lot of time dreaming up ways to be excused from this particular task. "I just don't have the spirit."

"Then find it." Nora's voice softened. "I don't mean to sound cruel and heartless. I'd feel the same way if I'd buried my husband the week before Christmas, but it's been three years. You have Joshua to think about. You don't want to deprive him of the excitement, do you?"

"He's only two. He won't realize what it's all about until he starts kindergarten."

Nora shook her head. "He watches television. This time next year he'll have marked every page in a Christmas catalog with what he wants from Santa. You might as well think of this as your first step. You're only decorating the waiting room, not the entire clinic or the courthouse square.''

''Don't forget the party.''

''Then sign up to be a greeter. Once everyone has arrived, you can slip out and no one will be the wiser.''

Of course, greeting people meant she'd have to appear with a smile on her face and spout the usual holiday platitudes to everyone who entered. She couldn't do that. She wouldn't.

Claire shook her head. ''I don't think so.''

Nora shrugged. ''You'd better volunteer for something or I can guarantee you'll be stuck guarding the eggnog. Believe me, that job lasts *all* night. There's always some jerk who wants to spike it.''

''A typical company party,'' Claire said, remembering those she'd attended with Ray.

''Complete with people who get loaded. Why do free drinks always bring out the closet alcoholics? Anyway, I'd better run. We have a busy morning ahead of us.''

Claire made one last attempt. ''Are you sure I can't talk you into taking over for me on the decorating detail?''

''Oh, you probably could,'' Nora began, but before Claire could feel relieved she added, ''if I thought this wouldn't be a good thing for you to do. As far as I'm concerned, this is the perfect Christmas prescription for your holiday blues, so you can save your breath.''

''Gee, thanks.''

Nora grinned. ''What are friends for? As an added bonus, you'll spend quality time with our delectable Dr Alex. Why, you might even have a conversation with him that doesn't revolve around patients or diseases.''

''We talk,'' Claire protested. Granted, their discussions usually centered around their children, but they did talk.

''Then I've given you another opportunity.''

''I'm going to scratch you off my Christmas card list,'' Claire warned.

"You don't send cards."

"I could start."

Nora giggled. "Trust me. This will be good for you. See you later."

Frustrated by Nora's logic, Claire rubbed the back of her neck and considered her choices. As far as she could tell, and much to her annoyance, she didn't have any.

"I'm going to write a list just so I can scratch Nora off," she mumbled aloud.

"Did I hear you mention a list?" Alex's familiar voice caught her by surprise.

"Christmas cards."

"Oh. I thought you might have remembered something we should buy."

"Not a thing."

"Shall we still plan on decorating this afternoon?"

She managed to stifle a resigned sigh. "Yeah, sure. Why not?" The sooner they finished, the sooner the weight on her chest would lift and she could breathe freely again.

"Are you sure you don't want to join our shopping expedition? We could use another opinion."

Claire should have told him that her trip to the beauty shop had fallen through, but the mere thought of holiday trimmings sent her stomach into a series of cartwheels. "I'm sure. Someone needs to organize things so we'll be ready to roll when you get back."

"Fair enough." He glanced at his watch. "Is it only eight-thirty?"

"It's nearly nine. When are you going to break down and buy a watch that works?"

"It only needs a new battery."

"You said that two batteries ago. Just go to the store and pick out a decent watch."

"I haven't found one I like. They're all so high-tech, it's impossible to tell time. Speaking of which, the

Harkness baby is coming in this morning. Make sure the lab faxes his morning bilirubin result.''

Medical business she could handle. ''Will do.''

Fifteen minutes later, she ushered Judy Weatherbee into the first exam room. The forty-two-year-old woman had come in for her weekly blood-pressure check, and after today Alex would decide if intervention was necessary. From the high figure—one forty-seven over ninety-eight—Claire suspected that he would.

''Are you feeling OK?'' she asked.

Judy shrugged. ''I'm fine, other than a slight headache. I don't know why my pressure is high. It never has been before.''

''Those figures have a tendency to creep up when we get older,'' Claire explained. ''Do you have any family history?''

Judy shook her head. ''We don't smoke, or drink either. If cancer doesn't get us, then we live to a ripe old age. All of my grandparents lived into their nineties.''

''That's a plus,'' she said.

''What will he do? Since my numbers don't seem to be coming down.''

''He'll probably start you on medication. Preventing a stroke or a heart attack is the goal. Not to worry, though.'' Claire patted her hand. ''We'll see what he says.''

In the end, Alex chose the very lowest dose of a beta-blocker and asked her to return in another week.

The rest of the morning was busy and Claire ran to and fro, trying to anticipate Alex's needs and follow his orders. Little Blake Harkness's bilirubin had come down, but it was still fourteen, which indicated that his liver hadn't completely kicked in yet. His mother was given instructions to keep him wrapped in his special space-age blanket that helped break down the bile pigment, giving him that yellow, glow-in-the-dark appearance.

The pace of any day preceding a holiday was hectic, but

the volume of work on this pre-Thanksgiving shift was worse because observing the occasion meant the clinic would be closed for the next four days. The cold November weather only added to the stress as patients who thought they were coming down with the usual winter ailments wanted a last-minute visit to the doctor while he was still available. Between those folks, the regularly scheduled appointments and cases like young Raven Ellison, who'd fallen off the monkey bars at recess and sprained his wrist, Claire hardly had time to think, much less fret over the task looming ahead.

She may have hidden her inner turmoil behind an upbeat attitude but now, with the patients gone, the staff at lunch and Alex leaving to pick up his daughter and embark on their shopping quest, she couldn't.

The box of last year's decorations, which she'd forced herself to open, brought back the overwhelming sense of loss.

You can do this, Claire. You really can.

She stroked the soft beard of the eighteen-inch-tall chubby-cheeked Santa in her hand and remembered how she'd once looked forward to this time of year. She used to love the winter celebrations with their hustle and bustle, but her eagerness was only a distant memory that belonged to another lifetime. It was amazing how one day, one hour, one minute, had made a world of difference in her attitude.

Think of it as just another holiday, like Valentine's Day, or Easter, or Independence Day.

How could she when the scent of the freshly cut, newly delivered evergreen standing in one corner of the patients' waiting room reminded her of the Ponderosa pine that stood sentinel over her husband's grave?

No, it wasn't just another holiday. It was the Christmas season, the season she started to dread when the leaves began to turn color and fall to the ground. Most people counted the days until December 25th but she counted them until the 26th—the day when the radio stations returned to their regular programming and everyone stopped greeting each other with the phrase that was so at odds with how she felt.

Merry Christmas.

For her, it might be Christmas, but it certainly wasn't "merry." This entire month reminded her of everything she and her son had lost, and not for the first time she wondered why someone, *somewhere* hadn't built a resort specifically for people like her who simply wanted to pass through these weeks as painlessly as possible.

Resolutely squaring her jaw, she set Santa on the end table next to the matching figure of Mrs Claus. No one, other than Nora, need know how painful this was for her. She would see this project through to its bitter end.

In the meantime, she'd hope that Nora's philosophy was right, that getting involved with holiday preparations in the professional atmosphere at work was a dress rehearsal for doing so at home. Joshua didn't deserve to miss what every other child was taking for granted. If she managed to decorate the office, then maybe, just maybe, she could cope with adding a few holiday touches to her own house.

Somewhat reassured by the thought, she returned to the man-sized red plastic storage tub that the maintenance crew had delivered earlier. As she unpacked the rest of its contents, she was relieved to find the odd assortment of generic items—strands of lights, boxes of shiny, multicolored ornaments, packages of silver icicles and garlands. Part of her reticence at decorating at home was because so many of her things held a special significance. Fortunately, none of the baubles in this box did, and she was supremely grateful.

Grateful, that was, until she opened a tan box without thinking. The sight of the ornate angel tree-topper lying in a bed of white tissue paper literally took her breath away.

It was an exact replica of hers, with its curly reddish-gold hair and the trim on its gold brocade gown. She stroked the red soutache braid, barely conscious of the cold sweat breaking across her forehead. Crowning the top of the tree with this was out of the question. She'd brave the crowds at the store and spend her own carefully budgeted funds to buy something else. A star, a Santa, *anything* could fill that spot, but not this particular angel which brought such bitter-sweet memories to mind.

Picturing a possible alternative, she didn't realize she had company until Alex interrupted her thoughts.

"Is everything OK?"

CHAPTER TWO

CLAIRE slammed the lid on the box and dropped it back in the plastic tub. Swallowing hard, she turned to gaze up at Alex and hoped that he hadn't noticed anything amiss.

To her dismay, a curious wrinkle had appeared on his high forehead and she recognized the question in his midnight-black eyes. Determined to divert his curiosity, she managed a reassuring smile. "Sure. Why do you ask?"

He shrugged, but the furrow didn't disappear. Funny thing, but his speculative gaze made her feel as if he could see into her very heart.

"You looked a little...tense," he finally said.

If "tense" was a polite way to say she looked as if she was in the middle of a panic attack, then he was right. She drew in a deep breath and prayed that her smile would appear sincere.

"Did I?" She cast around and tried to think of an excuse for the grim expression she'd obviously been wearing. "I was just going through the things we've used in years past." She motioned to the bags in his hand. "Did you find what you wanted?"

His chuckle was like a soothing balm to her stressed nerves. This man radiated calm, and at the moment she needed it as desperately as a diabetic needed insulin.

"And then some," he said. "Jennie insisted we buy lots of icicles. She claims it would look anemic if every branch wasn't dripping with them."

"Big word for a little girl."

He shrugged. "One of her friends' mothers took iron tablets and she asked me why. Anyway, when it comes to Christmas, there's no such thing as 'too much' of any-

20

thing.'' He grinned. ''She struggles to whittle her wish list down to her five most wanted things.''

So much for Claire's philosophy of ''less is more''. She'd be lucky if they finished today.

Realizing Alex was alone, she asked, ''Where is Jennie, by the way?''

''At the soda pop machine. She'll be here shortly. Before she arrives, though, I have a favor to ask.''

Alex rarely asked for favors—at least, he rarely asked *her.* On those few occasions, they'd been relatively minor requests, like dropping off a letter at the clinic's post office box outside in order to meet the pick-up deadline. Now the tentative note in his voice and obvious uncertainty suggested that this time his ''favor'' might not be a simple one.

On the other hand, it couldn't be worse than the task now facing her.

''Ask away.''

He rubbed one temple and she noticed the few threads of silver in his dark hair. ''Would you mind starting without me?''

''You can't desert me. You got us into this mess,'' she said, hoping she didn't sound as frantic as she felt. She'd hoped to hang in the background and watch Alex and Jennie work.

''I won't abandon you. I only need to look over a few reports and make a few phone calls that I can't put off.''

''We could wait.''

''I don't know how long I'll be.'' He glanced around the room. ''The patients probably wouldn't appreciate stepping over all this clutter.''

Trapped. That's how she felt. Utterly, totally, completely trapped.

''Knowing my daughter,'' he added, ''she'll probably want to do it all by herself, but if you could work together…?'' His voice trailed off as he raised one eyebrow in question. "Make sure she doesn't go overboard."

At eight, Jennie was more than capable of hanging ornaments by herself, but if it made him feel better to think they were working together, then so be it. As for going overboard…

"I get it," she said lightly. "You want me to play the heavy if she gets a hare-brained idea."

"Sort of, but not really. You see, at home we use everything we have, but no one sees it except us. This…" he glanced at the tree "…is being judged."

For herself, Claire didn't care about a contest, although she knew their tree would reflect good or bad on both her and Alex. For that she owed him the best job possible, even if she was being forced into it. "I'll try."

"Great." The worry in Alex's eyes faded and he glanced at his watch. "Where is she? It doesn't take this long to buy a fruit drink."

"Maybe she's eating a snack, too."

"Probably." He sighed as he rolled his eyes in apparent mock frustration. "It doesn't matter that she ate lunch forty minutes ago. There's some sort of psychological tie between the end of the school day and food. You'll see."

"I have a few years before I'll notice," she said.

"Joshua might be only two but, believe me, you'll blink and he'll be twelve," he assured her. "They don't stay babies forever."

"So true." Already Joshua was exerting his childish independence and it wouldn't be long before he'd prefer playing with his friends to being with his mother. Right now, she could meet his nurturing needs, but would she be enough for him when his interests turned to more masculine pursuits?

Worry about that later, she told herself. As her mother had advised, take one day at a time.

Before Alex could share more parental tidbits, his

daughter burst into the room carrying a shoe box, presumably filled with her hand-made snowflakes. Jennie's small face was wreathed in smiles and Claire once again noted how closely she resembled her father with her dark hair and eyes. She was a pretty child, which wasn't unexpected when one considered Alex's good looks. As far as Claire was concerned, the thin scar running from her nose to her mouth that marked every child born with a cleft lip was hardly noticeable. Her speech patterns suggested that her palate had been affected, too, but all in all she sounded quite normal.

She was also tall for her age and with her beautiful smile and thick eyelashes, she'd give Alex a few more gray hairs when boys started to notice the gem in their midst.

"Can we start now?" Jennie asked, unable to stand still in her excitement. "Can we?"

"Sure thing," Alex said as he tugged on Jennie's ponytail. "I'm going to work in my office for a while, but Claire's going to help."

The excitement on her face dimmed. Jennie pulled Alex aside and said in a loud whisper, "But, Dad, you said you would."

"And I will," he said firmly. "But first I have to clear my desk. You won't even notice I'm gone."

"But—" the little girl protested.

"But nothing. This is the way it is, and if you argue you won't help at all."

Jennie frowned, but held her tongue.

"Now, now. Claire won't bite." He looked over Jennie's bowed head to wink at her. "Remember, Claire's in charge."

"But, Daddy," Jennie wailed. "I drew it out so we'd know what to buy. If she doesn't like my idea, we can't change now."

Claire decided to step in. "Your father has told me all about your plans. I think they sound wonderful. Why don't you show me your drawing so I can picture the tree the way you do? Then we'll get busy.''

Somewhat appeased, Jennie pulled a folded piece of paper out of her jeans pocket. Claire sensed, rather than saw, Alex's stealthy departure, and she sent him a silent admonition to hurry back.

Jennie handed her the now unfolded scrap of paper. ''Daddy said this looked great.''

Knowing that she couldn't disagree, Claire studied the colored artwork, complete with both large and small snow-flakes and frosted glass icicles. To her surprise, she didn't want to. ''This is really good. I wouldn't change a thing.''

Jennie grinned. ''Really?''

''You've thought this out well. I do have a suggestion, though. Blue is a cool color, so why don't we add shiny blue balls for a little extra sparkle?''

''OK.''

The decision made and tragedy averted, Claire injected as much enthusiasm as she could muster into her voice and squared her shoulders. ''Where should we start?''

''You're in charge,'' Jennie reminded her, as if Claire had forgotten their hierarchy.

''Ah, but that doesn't mean I can't listen to my helper's ideas.''

''My dad always puts the lights on first.''

''Of course. How could I forget? Do you want to handle that by yourself?''

Jennie studied the tree for a moment. ''I'm not tall enough to reach the top. Not yet, anyway.''

Fortunately, the strand of lights Claire had chosen was in working order and it didn't take long for her to position it to Jennie's satisfaction.

''What's next?'' Claire asked.

''The ornaments,'' Jennie informed her importantly.

''Snowflakes and icicles. Why don't I dig them out of

their packages and you can hang them wherever you'd like?"

"OK."

Claire removed the cartons from the plastic sacks Alex had carried in while Jennie threaded the wire hangers through the holes on her paper snowflakes.

"Your little boy is cute," Jennie commented. "I saw him the other day when you were outside. It looked like he was having a good time playing in the leaves."

Claire remembered. They had spent all day Saturday doing yard work. She had raked and Joshua had spent his time destroying her piles. "He did."

"I bet he'll love seeing the Christmas lights."

"I'm sure he will." She'd drive him through their neighborhood and the park when the weather co-operated so he could see the elaborate display that was touted as being the largest in the county. Fortunately, he was still too young to wonder why they wouldn't have Santas and snowmen in front of their house when the majority of people did.

"We're going to buy our tree on Friday," Jennie went on.

"That's nice."

"Do you have a real tree or an artificial one?"

Claire wasn't sure how to answer. "Neither." At Jennie's puzzlement, she added, "I haven't had a tree for a few years."

"You haven't?"

"No." She changed the conversation with a falsely bright tone. "Would you look at that? We've used all the wire hangers. I'll look in the box for more."

"OK."

Claire was glad she'd diverted Jennie's attention, but as soon as she returned with an unopened package, Jennie asked, "Why don't you have a Christmas tree?"

How could she make Jennie understand why the season

didn't give her the joy it gave everyone else? "It's a lot of work for Joshua and me."

"Doesn't Joshua's daddy help you?"

"He's in heaven."

"Ah," Jennie said in an understanding way. Then, just as Claire was certain she had accepted her explanation, the youngster kept going. "My dad and I are by ourselves and we don't think it's too much work."

How could she counter that? "Yes, but you're not a baby. You can handle most of the job on your own."

"Except for the top."

"Except for the top," Claire agreed.

Jennie looked thoughtful as she hung another ornament. "Babies aren't much help, I suppose. They're always in the way, too."

"That's right."

"Does Joshua have a grandma or a grandpa who could watch him?"

"Yes, but they live in San Francisco and we don't see them often. What about you?"

"My grandma lives here. My dad grew up in Pleasant Valley, but they moved away when he was thirteen. After my grandpa died, my grandma came back. Last year, Daddy decided to move here, too, so Grandma wouldn't be by herself."

"I'm sure she was glad you did."

Jennie nodded. "It's me, my dad and grandma. Oh, and Mrs Rowe. She's the housekeeper."

"How nice for you to have so many people taking care of you."

"Yup. Some of my friends have stepmoms and stepdads, but I don't need one. I'm practically grown up."

Claire hid a smile. "I can see that."

Jennie stood on tiptoe to hang a snowflake, but she couldn't reach the uppermost branches. She tried several times, before giving up.

Claire wondered if she should volunteer, but Jennie seemed determined to accomplish as much as she could on her own. Alex had made it plain that Claire played an integral part in this project, too, but Jennie clearly didn't want anyone usurping her father's duties.

It became more apparent when Jennie dragged a chair close to the tree and stood on the seat cushion. After placing a snowflake on the highest limb, she beamed triumphantly before she jumped down to select a glass icicle. Before she could climb on her makeshift stool again, Claire stopped her.

"If you fall and hurt yourself, we'll both be in trouble," she told Jennie.

"I won't fall."

"Probably not," Claire agreed, "but accidents happen. You wouldn't want to break your arm or leg, though. You'd miss out on a lot of fun."

Jennie frowned. "But I can't reach high enough."

"Do what you can with both feet on the ground," Claire advised. "Your father can help with the rest when he comes back. He should be here shortly." She hoped.

"OK." Suddenly, Jennie hesitated. "You could probably do the top."

Claire sensed how difficult it had been for the youngster to offer. It was just as difficult for her to accept. "If your dad hasn't returned by the time you've finished the rest of the tree, then I will. In the meantime, I'll supervise."

Satisfied with Claire's answer, Jennie resumed her duties while Claire watched and tried not to remember her own tree-decorating occasions. She and Ray would spend hours good-naturedly arguing over where to place each ornament while they drank hot apple cider and ate the shortbread cookies she traditionally bought for this special day.

Could she go through the motions alone this year, with only Joshua for company?

She would, she determined, but on a much smaller scale than before. A stocking for Joshua, a few twinkly lights on the mantel and a twelve-inch, no-assembly-or-decorating-required fiber-optic tree would provide all the holiday cheer she needed or could tolerate.

It might not be much, but it was better than nothing.

Alex ambled out of his office, determined to let another five minutes pass before he joined Jennie and Claire. His excuse for paperwork had been just that—an excuse—but he had his reasons. Jennie's teacher had mentioned at their last conference that she was extremely territorial and needed to work on what Mrs Vincent called a "team attitude".

He'd known that she preferred having things her way— what child didn't?—but he assumed her disposition was due to a double dose of the "onlies". Being an only child of an only parent was a drawback when it came time to learn about sharing and compromise.

As the years had marched on, he'd thought she'd outgrown that phase, but Mrs Vincent's comment proved otherwise. For a man who prided himself on his powers of observation, it had been a humbling pill to swallow.

Which brought him to the Christmas tree issue. Perhaps if Jennie had to work with someone who wasn't as interior-design-challenged as he was, she might learn the fine art of compromise. Now he wondered if he should have fully explained his plan before thrusting Claire in the middle of it.

He quickened his step, then halted in the doorway to survey the scene. Claire was busy tidying the room while his daughter happily hung her snowflakes.

Alex should have joined them, but he wanted to see how the two interacted almost as much as he wanted to feast his eyes on the woman he'd hired.

Claire was taller than most women, attractive and had

short straight, coppery-colored hair. Her voice was always calm and soothing and, no matter how stressed his day was, a few minutes in her presence lifted his mood more effectively than anything money could buy.

She was slender, and he suspected that Joshua would grow up with the same build. Today she wore a scrub suit with kittens of all shades playing with an assortment of yarn. Idly, he wondered where she found her uniforms because the fabric designs were so different from everyone else's.

He started forward, but her expression made him hesitate. She looked almost…grim, as if the chore was more detestable than fun.

He realized something else. Claire and his daughter weren't working together, as he'd imagined.

So much for his carefully thought-out plan.

He strode in and used his most hearty voice to disguise his disappointment. "How are you two ladies coming along?"

"Fine, Daddy. I saved the space at the top for you."

He eyed the bare branches that were far beyond Jennie's reach but well within Claire's. "Jennie," he warned, "you were supposed to let Claire help."

"I know," Jennie assured him with wide eyes. "But she said to save those for you. If you didn't come back soon, then she would do your part."

"It's true," Claire chimed in as she placed another box that Jennie had emptied into the storage crate. "I volunteered to be a technical consultant until you arrived. With her eye for detail, it seemed a shame to stand in the way of a creative genius."

Jennie preened under Claire's praise, and it was obvious that Claire had won a new friend in his daughter. Perhaps his plan hadn't completely backfired.

"See, Dad? Everything turned out fine. So hurry up. I can't wait to see how it looks when it's finished."

"It's already beautiful," he said loyally, "but I'll hurry." He glanced around. "Where are the snowflakes?"

"I'll get them." Jennie chose one from her box and handed it to him. "Put it in that spot, right there." She pointed to an upper limb.

"Here?"

"A little more to the left."

With the paper ornament in place to Jennie's satisfaction, she handed him another. Once again, she gave him specific directions.

"Bossy-boots, aren't we?" he teased.

Jennie rolled her eyes. "Don't you want our tree to be *perfect,* so we win a prize? Maybe it will be a trip to Disney World."

"Sorry, kiddo, but the prize is a luncheon sandwich platter for the entire department. Vacations to Disney World or Disney Land aren't part of the package."

"Oh." Her expression sobered. "Well, it'd still be a good thing if we won, wouldn't it?"

"You bet. In the meantime…" he jiggled a snowflake above her head "…we'd better finish this job before the patients start arriving on the doorstep."

"OK." He reached toward a branch, but Jennie stopped him. "Not there, Daddy. Move it a little closer to the blue ball."

"Yes, Alex. Do pay attention." Claire's eyes sparkled with humor.

He faked a groan. "How lucky can a man get to have two women telling him what to do and how to do it?"

"Extremely lucky," Claire replied. "It isn't every fellow who has the honor of working with two talented artists—right, Jennie?"

Jennie giggled, and for the next ten minutes Alex did his best to satisfy both, although his daughter was definitely the more demanding of the two. Finally, the evergreen was covered with carefully positioned ornaments.

Throughout the entire process, Alex was conscious of Claire as she stood in the background, offering only an occasional comment. At one point she moved toward the window and stared into the parking lot as if distancing herself from their project.

He couldn't imagine what had grabbed her attention. Their five-physician family practice waiting room boasted a view of the parking lot. His view, however, revealed a beautiful woman with whom any man would be proud to be seen, himself included.

"Something's missing," Jennie announced.

Alex took his mind off Claire and focused on the tree. "It looks good to me. What do you think, Claire?"

She turned from the window to study the pine. "Something *is* missing," she finally said.

"I thought so," Jennie said importantly. "But what?"

"I'm not sure, but if we think about it, I'm sure we'll figure out the problem." Then, to Alex's surprise, she turned to stare out the window again.

"Must be something interesting out there," he joked.

"There is," she commented. "Either we have a driver who can't drive, or..." She stopped short.

"What's wrong?"

"Someone just parked on the sidewalk. It's a woman and she's— Oh, my."

"She's what?" He started to see for himself, but Claire was already rushing to the door.

"A woman is carrying in a child," she said crisply. "He's limp. Maybe unconscious."

CHAPTER THREE

CLAIRE met the lady at the door with Alex at her side. "What's wrong?"

"She's choking." The woman, in her mid-twenties, could hardly speak coherently. "Please help her."

Wordlessly, Alex took the child. It was obvious from the little girl's struggle to gasp air and the bluish tinge to her lips that she was in trouble.

Claire had performed the Heimlich maneuver on one occasion, but in that instance it had involved an adult and the situation hadn't been as advanced as this. How fortunate they were to have Alex on the scene.

His first attempt was unsuccessful and the four-year-old hung over his arm like a rag doll.

The woman moaned. "Shouldn't we find a doctor?"

"You have," Claire assured her. "This is Dr Ridgeway. He's a family practice physician. While he's working on your daughter, tell us what happened."

"Mandy's my niece, not my daughter. I'm Rebecca Hollister."

She drew a shaky hand through her blonde hair, cut in sleek lines that suggested a trendy stylist. Her clothes were clearly designer label and Claire sensed that her experience with children was limited. Her story confirmed it.

"I'm looking after Mandy today while my sister and her husband are Christmas shopping. We went to the convenience store to fill my gas tank and I bought Mandy some candy. We hadn't gone more than a few blocks before she started choking."

Alex performed several more compressions to Mandy's

diaphragm and suddenly a small piece of hard green candy shot across the floor.

Mandy immediately began gulping air as tears brimmed in her blue eyes. Although Claire held the utmost faith in Alex's ability to turn the situation around, it was still a relief to fix the problem without resorting to more drastic medical measures.

"Cool," Jennie said in the background.

"Oh, thank you," Rebecca said, shaky. "Thank you so much."

"Why don't we go into the waiting room to give Mandy a chance to recover?" Claire suggested.

"Good idea," Alex said. Once inside, he sat on the nearest chair with the youngster on his lap. "You're going to be fine," he said softly as he rubbed circles on her back. Mandy was too worn out to protest, but Claire didn't think she would have, even if she'd been able. Something about Alex seemed to inspire instant confidence from his young patients, and Mandy was clearly no exception.

As Claire watched him give his calm attention, she understood why Jennie thought the sun rose and set on her father. He was clearly a natural at this parenting business. Regret that her own son wouldn't experience the same touch pierced her for a moment before she chased the fruitless emotion away. Fate had dealt this hand to them and she and Joshua would manage like countless other people in a similar situation.

Rebecca hovered over Alex. "I can't thank you enough. I don't know what I would have done if I hadn't seen the sign and pulled in for help. I live out of town, so I didn't know where to find the hospital."

"You're not far. It's only three blocks away," Claire said. "If you stay on this road, you'll run into it."

"It's a good thing you stopped here, though," Alex said. "With a blocked airway, time is crucial."

Mandy, obviously recovered from her ordeal, slipped off Alex's knee and stood by her aunt. "I'm OK now."

Rebecca crouched down and hugged her. "Are you sure?"

Mandy nodded. "I'm hungry."

Alex laughed. "She's definitely going to be fine."

Rebecca straightened. "What do I owe you?"

"Nothing," he said. "Just drive home carefully. And don't give her any more big pieces of candy."

"Believe me, I won't. My sister is going to pitch a fit when I tell her what happened." She looked guilty. "She doesn't allow Mandy to eat sweets, so I won't be in her good graces for a while. Ah, well. Better to have her scold me for breaking her candy rule than hating me because Mandy..." She glanced at her niece. "Well, you know what I mean."

Claire smiled. "We do, and you're right."

"That was really neat," Jennie exclaimed after Rebecca and Mandy had left. "Do you do stuff like that all the time?"

Alex laughed aloud as he smiled at his daughter. "Our days usually aren't so exciting."

"Speaking of exciting," Claire said, "we need to hurry and tidy the waiting room. Our patients will be arriving soon."

"We still haven't figured out what's missing," Jennie reminded them.

"Maybe we'll find something in the crate," Alex replied. "Let's look."

Jennie held up a strand of gold beads. "What about these?"

"Silver would be perfect, but not gold," Claire said as she rummaged through bags of red braid, colorful beads and ribbon in every color imaginable.

Suddenly, Jennie squealed. "Oh, isn't she beautiful?"

Claire glanced at what held Jennie so enthralled, and her

heart seemed to skip a beat. She'd opened the box containing the angel.

"Can we use her?" Jennie asked.

"We bought a lighted snowflake," Alex pointed out.

"A tree should have an angel on the top," she insisted. "It's tradition."

"The snowflake would look better because of the other snowflakes on the tree," Claire said, trying to be her most convincing.

"Maybe the angel is what our tree needs," Jennie said hopefully.

Alex shook his head. "The snowflake stays."

"I still think the angel should go on the top," Jennie whined as she stroked the figure nestled in tissue paper. "Especially because she looks like you." She lifted it up to show her father. "See?"

"She does," Alex said in amazement. "The hair's longer, but otherwise the resemblance is uncanny."

Claire didn't need to look at the tree-topper to know that the angel's tresses matched her own coppery shade. Three years ago, Ray had seen the similarity and had insisted on buying the angel because of it.

"An angel on the tree and one in my arms," he'd teased her. "What more could a man want?"

She forced the bitter-sweet memory aside. "What a coincidence."

"Are you sure we can't use her?" Jennie wheedled.

Alex took it out of the box to examine it more closely. "It stands by itself. Why don't we set her on the table instead?"

"OK," Jennie acquiesced, "but she really belongs on the tree."

"Maybe next year."

With luck, someone else in the department would have this dubious honor, not Claire.

"It's still missing something," Jennie reminded them.

"The judging doesn't take place until Monday, so we have a few more days for inspiration to strike," Alex said. "As for me, I think you two have done a fantastic job."

Jennie giggled as she preened under his praise. "Is it good enough to win the prize?"

"I'm sure of it. Wouldn't you agree, Claire?"

"Without a doubt," she answered.

Although she said the right words, her voice sounded as strained as her smile. Before Alex could ask what was bothering her, she changed the subject. "Would you look at the time? I'd better call Maintenance to move this carton before our patients trip over it this afternoon."

With that, she hurried away. Now perplexed, Alex watched her go.

"How come she was in such a rush, Dad?"

Alex wasn't going to speculate on Claire's behavior with his daughter. "She has a lot to do before we're open for business. Everything has to be in order."

"Oh." Satisfied by his explanation, Jennie adjusted one of her snowflakes.

Alex's thoughts drifted back to his new nurse. Claire had been a refreshing change from his previous assistant. Rosemary Diaz had been a competent nurse, but organization hadn't been part of her vocabulary. How they'd functioned as well as they had was what he still considered an unsolved mystery.

He'd never quite understood Rosemary's idea of order, or if she even knew what it meant. By contrast, Claire placed the paperwork in the appropriate in, out or review basket and neatly arranged their supplies in labeled drawers. He could actually find things for himself without feeling helpless or frustrated in his own domain. His day simply ran more smoothly.

He liked being with Claire, and not just in their doctor-nurse roles. Quite by chance, one day several weeks ago, he'd gone to the clinic's employee cafeteria to grab a sandwich from the vending machine and had seen Claire sitting by herself. He'd joined her and had enjoyed himself so much that he'd made a point to "drop in" on Wednesdays ever since.

Those thirty minutes of conversation always rejuvenated him, although, come to think about it, she didn't say too much about herself. From her interview, he knew she was twenty-nine, widowed and supported a two-year-old son. She was good friends with Dennis's nurse, Nora Laslow, and had applied for the opening as soon as Rosemary had followed her husband to Arizona. On the other hand, Claire spoke about Joshua quite often and he knew as much about him as he did his own daughter.

He'd considered taking things to the next level and asking her to dinner and a movie, but his courage had always failed him. She'd never treated him any differently than she treated the other men in the practice—single, or married—so, if she wasn't as interested in him as he was her, asking her out could cause all sorts of problems.

Yes, he was glad Claire's path was intertwined with his, but during his more lonely moments he wished that she worked for one of his partners. It would certainly simplify matters...

Jennie interrupted his wayward thoughts. "I don't think she likes Christmas."

"What makes you say that?"

"She didn't seem excited about decorating the tree."

"She didn't, did she?" he mused. When he'd first mentioned the task, he'd expected Claire to grumble and groan—who wouldn't when the stakes were high and her schedule was full?—but she'd seemed to accept her lot. Now, when he added her response to the angel in the box, that reluctance took on greater significance than simply being too busy. Perhaps if he hadn't been so eager to be with her, he would have been more attuned to the signals she'd been sending.

Jennie shook her head. "She doesn't have one at her house either."

"Some people don't." In his circle of friends, he didn't know of a single person who didn't set up a tree—even a small one—but there were bound to be a few in the world who didn't bother. Claire didn't seem the type of person who shunned the holidays, but with her husband gone she probably found this to be a difficult time of year.

"She used to have one. Now she says it's too much work. I don't think it's work, do you?"

"It does take time and effort," he said, "so you could call it work."

"But, Dad, it's *fun.*"

Alex lightly chucked Jennie's chin. "It is, at that. Speaking of work, I have my own waiting for me and you, young lady, need to finish your school assignments."

"But, Dad, I have *four* whole days to do my math."

"Those four days will go fast, and if you don't have homework hanging over your head, you'll enjoy your vacation that much more. No arguments."

Jennie rolled her eyes and slumped her shoulders. "OK," she said in her most long-suffering voice. "You will hurry so we can leave early, won't you?"

"I'll do my best," he promised. As he returned to his office and the reports awaiting him, he wondered what he could do to help Claire survive the season. She was too young and too full of vitality to be a Christmas Scrooge.

Claire took refuge in their medical records room, thankful that the holiday spirit hadn't entered this domain. Filing patient records was the sort of mindless activity she needed while she recovered from the strain of pretending that all was well. Although it was their receptionist's job to file the records, she'd been desperate for something to do and a harried office clerk had gratefully accepted her offer.

"Roberta said I'd find you in here." Nora sauntered down Claire's aisle. "How did it go?"

"How did what go?"

Nora chortled. "You know what I mean. Come on, tell me how the decorating went."

Claire pretended nonchalance. "Fine. Jennie and Alex hung the ornaments while I served as technical advisor and person in charge of clean-up. The tree in the waiting room is officially decked out in Christmas cheer."

"No bad moments?"

She glanced at Nora fondly. Her friend had a heart as big as Texas, from where she hailed, and nosiness to match. Although her birthday was a week before Claire's, on occasion she acted like the bossy older sister Claire had never had. Claire tried not to mind because she knew Nora meant well.

"A few, but I lived to tell the tale."

"And how was spending time with Alex?" Nora asked with a sly wink.

"How was it supposed to be? We were in a medical office waiting room with his daughter."

Nora sighed. "Too bad."

"You shouldn't be matchmaking," Claire said offhandedly. If Nora even suspected that it took all of Claire's concentration to act like a responsible mother when a single glance from him made her want to revert to her carefree single days, she'd never let up.

"What else can a married gal do for her single friends?"

"I don't know, but I'll think of something."

Nora crossed her arms and leaned against the shelving unit. "You've worked with Alex for nearly two months. What do you think of our good doctor?"

"He's a fantastic physician."

"I wasn't referring to his medical skills."

Claire grinned. "I know."

"He's quite a hunk, isn't he?"

"You're not supposed to notice things like that," Claire chided gently. "What would Carter think?"

"I'm only enjoying Mother Nature's handiwork," Nora protested. "There's nothing wrong with that. But you still haven't answered my question."

"He's very…" Claire couldn't think of the right word to describe him. She only knew that a spark of awareness vibrated in the air when he was nearby—a spark that she found strangely disconcerting. He certainly wasn't the first male she'd come in contact with since Ray's death. She'd worked with physicians, dealt with patients and been introduced to prospective dates by well-meaning friends, but none of those fellows had caused her pulse to hum or charge the air with static electricity. None of their glances made her feel as if she were surrounded by flames either.

"Powerful," she finally decided.

"Does he make your toes tingle when he smiles at you?"

Heaven help her, but he did. His small courtesies had also reminded her of how much she missed the intimate companionship she'd grown accustomed to in her marriage.

"I'm sure he makes everyone's toes tingle," she evaded as she moved down the aisle to slip another folder into its proper place.

"Not mine. Maybe one or two," Nora corrected. "But it's nice to know that he affects all ten of yours."

"I didn't say that."

"Oh, Claire, you didn't have to. I can see it on your face."

"You're imagining things."

"Am I? Say, what job have you decided to tackle for the Christmas party?"

Claire was grateful that Nora had let the subject of her tingling toes drop. Alex may have managed to make her feel like a desirable woman instead of a sexless colleague, but for now she was content to hug that knowledge to herself. Heaven only knew what her friend would do with that information in her matchmaking arsenal.

As for the clinic's holiday bash, if other people wanted to observe the season in the usual bright and carefree manner they could, but she wouldn't tarnish Ray's memory in such a way. Her deceased husband and the holiday were too intertwined for her to separate so easily.

"I haven't given it much thought," she said. "Being on the clean-up crew might work. I could drop in after the festivities wind down. Or, since the party's on Saturday night, we could do the clean-up on Sunday. Then I wouldn't have to worry about finding a sitter for Joshua at one a.m."

"You'll have to pop in at some point in the evening."

"Hundreds of people are attending. No one will notice if I don't."

"Dr Grieg will and so will everyone else in our group. It'll be good for you."

"Spinach and liver are good for me, too, but I've managed to live without both quite nicely for nearly thirty years."

"You're putting the past behind you and looking forward, remember?"

Claire sighed. "I am, but I wasn't referring to parties when I said that."

"Doesn't matter. It's all part of the process."

"If you're going to use my own words against me every time you want me to do something…" Claire finished on a warning note.

"Hey, you gave me the weapon and I intend to use it." Nora sobered. "I also recall you asking me to keep you from changing your mind. I'm only honoring my part of our bargain. If it makes you feel better, though, don't think of it as a party. Think of it as a medical in-service with expensive refreshments."

"Yeah, right."

"You attend functions during the other eleven months of the year. Why not in December?"

"Because I can't," she answered flatly. Those gatherings didn't make her feel as if she were celebrating Ray's death. In her head, she knew she wasn't doing that, but in her heart, it felt that way.

"Ray's parents aren't here to pass judgment on you. Just because they turn into hermits for the entire holiday season doesn't mean you have to, too. You can't live your life to please them."

Claire managed a smile under Nora's sharp-eyed gaze. "I know, and I'm not. Granted, Marion wouldn't be happy if she thought I was traipsing from party to party, but I'm not staying at home because of her. I'm simply not ready to go."

"The longer you put this off, the harder it will be," Nora warned.

Claire shrugged. "Some things can't be rushed."

Roberta appeared at the end of their aisle. Her graying hair was in its perpetual state of dishevelment, although Claire suspected that if she constantly answered the phone and dealt with a myriad of details at once, she'd look frazzled, too.

"Speaking of being rushed, do you two realize that I have a room full of patients waiting to see a doctor? Some of us would like to go home before dark."

"Sorry." Claire slotted in the last folder. "We're on our way."

A few minutes later, she ushered a fifty-nine-year-old woman into an exam room. "What can we do for you today, Mrs O'Brien?"

Doris O'Brien was a well-dressed woman who looked twenty years younger than she was, thanks to plastic surgery. As a real-estate agent, she'd helped Claire find the house she'd eventually bought.

"Something is terribly wrong with me," she confessed. "Ever since I've been taking those pills to lower my cholesterol, I've been feeling poorly."

"How so?"

"My joints ache. I can't sleep at night. I'm absolutely exhausted. I simply can't function and I don't like it."

"Are you under any unusual stress?"

"Who isn't at this time of year?"

"More than the ordinary," Claire corrected.

"No. What's giving me stress is the fact that I'm not able to do what I normally do."

Claire jotted down a few notes. "In that case, I'll take a few readings and send the doctor in."

Doris's blood pressure, pulse and temperature were all normal, so after Claire had recorded those figures she summoned their next patient.

"Eddie!" she exclaimed when she saw the woman's familiar face. "You haven't had that baby yet?" Edwina Butler was a brunette who at thirty-five was having her first child. Actually, it wasn't her first because she'd miscarried at four months on two previous occasions, but this time she'd made it to thirty-six weeks, and everyone was collectively holding their breaths.

Eddie, as she preferred to be called, grinned. "I'm getting close. Last week Dr Ridgeway said 'any day', so I'm hoping I won't go past my due date."

Her husband, Joe, helped her step onto the scale. He'd accompanied his wife on every prenatal visit so far, which made him special in Claire's eyes. She'd never seen a man more solicitous of his pregnant wife but, then, he had reason to be. He wanted this baby as much as Eddie did.

"That makes two of us," he said. "The anticipation is about to kill me." His grin suggested otherwise.

"Good news," Claire said as she read the display. "You haven't gained any weight. You must have cut out the ice cream."

"She has," Joe said.

"Only because he made me," Eddie groused. "I'm living on lettuce and water. Joe's under strict orders to bring a five-pound box of chocolates after the baby comes."

"What? No red roses?" Claire teased as she led them into the room they reserved for expectant mothers.

"No." Eddie was adamant. "It's chocolate or he'd better stay at home."

"Did you hear that, Joe?" Claire asked.

Joe grinned. "I heard."

Claire quickly took Eddie's blood pressure. "Everything looks good from where I'm standing. Is the baby moving a lot?"

Eddie rubbed her tummy. "All the time. She's a regular wiggle worm."

"*He's* a track star," Joe corrected.

"You don't know the baby's sex?"

Eddie shook her head. "We don't want to know either. If something goes wrong…"

"We're going to do our best to avoid that," Claire reassured her. "Now, lie down and I'll send the doctor in."

The rest of the afternoon passed quickly. Doris O'Brien left with a different drug prescription, Eddie was sent home with admonitions to rest, and a variety of people who were all suffering from the latest round of chest colds, bronchitis and pneumonia were treated. By four o'clock, the waiting room was clear and Claire was straightening the exam rooms in preparation for Monday's patients.

In the meantime, she had four days at home to spoil Joshua.

She walked past Alex's office and saw Jennie seated behind his desk, her tongue peeking out of her mouth as she diligently wrote on a piece of paper.

Claire stopped in the doorway. "Is your dad around?"

"He went to talk to Dr Rehman."

"I see."

"Are you going home now?" Jennie asked.

"Yes. Have a happy Thanksgiving."

"Before you go, could you help me spell a word?"

"Sure. What is it?"

"Siamese. I want a Siamese kitten for Christmas, like those on your shirt."

Claire remembered Alex's comment about Jennie's lengthy wish list and wondered if Santa would be bringing kitty litter to the Ridgeway household. "Does your dad know you want a cat in your stocking?"

"He will after I write it down."

Claire crossed the room to stand in front of the desk. Alex had been right—Jennie's list had at least two dozen items on it, although several had been crossed off. "Are you ready?" At Jennie's nod, Claire spelt the word.

"Thanks," Jennie said as she replaced the cap on her pen. "I hope I get a kitty like the yellow one on your shirt, but I like the brown and black ones, too."

"They are cute, aren't they?"

Jennie nodded. "I haven't seen anyone with a shirt like yours before. Where did you get it?"

"I made it."

Her eyes widened. "You did? Wow."

"Thanks." Out of the corner of her eye, she saw Alex enter.

"Are you two ready to call it a day?" he asked.

"Definitely," Claire answered.

"Guess what, Dad?" Jennie asked. "Did you know that Claire sews her own clothes?"

His appreciative gaze rolled down her body, making her feel selfconscious. "I'm impressed," he drawled.

"Thanks." She hoped the surge of heat she felt wasn't obvious to anyone but her.

Jennie turned a hopeful gaze on Claire. "We've been wanting to hire someone to make my angel outfit for the school's Winter pageant. Could you?"

"I'm not a professional," Claire began, intending to refuse.

"If you can sew that..." Alex pointed to her tunic "...you're an expert in my books. The question is, would you have time? I know how busy everyone is right now."

Finding the few hours to take on this project wasn't the problem. Her own Christmas to-do list was painfully short and could be completed in an afternoon.

"Please?" Jennie begged. "We've asked and asked, and haven't found anyone. I need it in three weeks."

"What about the other mothers?"

Alex shook his head. "Most of them are in the same boat we are. I've already asked Nora, but she's swamped. My only other option is to borrow a white uniform from Hattie."

They *were* in dire straits if he was desperate enough to consider Hattie's old dress, circa the 1970s. Indecision gnawed at her.

What harm would sewing a costume do? her little voice asked.

What harm, indeed?

The real problem was that she felt like a bug trapped in a web with no way out, but she'd be a real Scrooge if she refused to spend a few hours stitching a couple of measly seams. The pageant was too important an event in Jennie's young life for her to look like a child playing dress-up in an outdated garment. Claire might not enjoy the holiday, but she couldn't spoil the season for someone else.

"I'll do it," she said simply.

CHAPTER FOUR

ON FRIDAY morning, Claire sat on the floor in one corner of her spare bedroom/sewing room and stacked blocks with Joshua while she kept one eye on the clock. It was nearly ten—the hour she'd agreed to meet with Alex and his daughter to work on Jennie's costume—and Claire had been playing with Joshua for the last thirty minutes. When her two guests arrived, she hoped he'd be content to watch one of his videos rather than demand to be the center of attention.

"Take your time," she told him as he placed one block on top of their pile in concentration so fierce that the tip of his tongue peeked out of his mouth. He didn't have the control he needed in his small fingers to set the block on straight, so the tower wobbled and wiggled before it finally toppled.

Joshua laughed aloud and clapped. "Uh-oh."

Claire leaned over to impulsively hug him and ruffle his baby-fine reddish-blond hair. "Uh-oh," she sing-songed with him. "It fell over. Are you tired of this or shall we play another game?"

He shook his head and wrinkled his brow in a manner very reminiscent of his father. "Again."

Claire glanced at the clock and decided she could indulge him. "Once more."

"More," Joshua demanded as he stacked two blocks on top of each other.

Claire obliged with her own contribution and allowed her mind to wander while he carefully engineered his tower. As reluctant as she'd been to sew Jennie's costume initially, she'd started thinking of it as simply a sewing

47

project. A few seams, a bit of trim and, presto, it would be ready. For what it was worth, she was almost excited because she wanted to transform Jennie into the most fabulous angel on stage.

No, Jennie's project wasn't a concern. Alex's presence in her home was. The clinic, with its hustle, bustle and professional atmosphere, insulated her from his forceful personality to a certain degree, but here the lines separating them would vanish. She'd see a completely different side to him.

It would be the side she'd caught glimpses of when he shared a spur-of-the-moment lunch-break. A side that made her see him more as a handsome man than a skilled physician.

A side that made her wish things she shouldn't.

The fact was, she'd enjoyed being married. She'd liked seeing trousers hanging in the closet next to her skirts and dresses. She didn't mind extra-large undershirts mingling with her undies in the washing machine and she'd looked forward to preparing meals for someone with more refined taste than Joshua.

Ray's death had left her adrift in more ways than one, but she'd slowly found her footing. While she would like to share her life with someone again, she refused to rush into anything. After enjoying one wonderful marriage, she wasn't going to settle for anything less, although she doubted if fate granted a person two such experiences in one's span of years.

By the time their tower had grown to the height of six blocks, the doorbell rang its melodious chorus of Westminster chimes.

Joshua's eyes widened at the sound and his eyes lit up with curiosity. He was smart enough to associate the tune with a visitor and, being a gregarious sort, he immediately clambered to his feet and waited for her to do the same.

"Door?" he asked.

"Someone's at the door," Claire agreed. "Stay here."

He stared at her with eyes glowing with eagerness and she knew he wouldn't obey. To him, the doorbell usually signaled someone new to play with and he didn't intend to delay his opportunity.

"Bell." His tone was urgent as he scurried out of the room.

Claire caught up with him in the living room, swept him onto one hip and hurried to greet her visitors.

"You're right on time," she told Jennie and Alex as she welcomed them inside, already noticing how small the foyer seemed with Alex standing in the middle of it.

"Daddy hates to be late," Jennie said.

"I know. May I take your coats?"

Joshua tugged on her sweatshirt. "Play?"

"No, we're not going to play," Claire told him firmly, tugging her neckline out of his grip. "We're going to work in Mommy's sewing room."

"Sew?" he asked.

"I should have called before we came, because we have a problem," Alex interrupted. "Her teacher said to make an angel costume, but didn't give any other instructions. I know you need fabric, but when we went to the store, Jennie and I disagreed on what would make a good costume. So we decided to get your opinion before we bought the wrong thing."

Claire suddenly noticed their empty hands. "You need a pattern and white material, probably cotton."

"There's cotton, cotton blends, muslin and fabric I haven't heard of," he confessed. "I was definitely out of my element and, to be honest, I didn't think it would be this difficult."

She gave him brownie points for braving this domain in the first place and tallied an extra one for admitting his inadequacy.

"Did you ask one of the clerks?" she asked. "They're usually very helpful."

"We were going to," Jennie piped up, "but she had a lot of customers. We waited in line for a long time and Daddy got impatient."

Claire grinned, imagining a frustrated Alex surrounded by a horde of women who had probably been tossing ideas back and forth about their sewing projects. She knew, because she'd done the same thing on many occasions.

"He finally gave up and said we should ask you," Jennie finished. "So can you help us?"

Claire hadn't expected this development, although from the way her luck seemed to be running she should have. "I'm going later this weekend," she offered, mentally reviewing her own list of depleted household essentials. "I'll buy what we need then."

Jennie's lip quivered. "Then I won't get to pick out anything?"

Claire wanted to point out that her choice was between white cotton and white cotton, but it was obviously important to Jennie to be involved from start to finish. "You're right. Choosing fabric is a difficult job. We'll go on Saturday."

Jennie shook her head. "Tomorrow won't work. We're getting our house ready for Christmas this afternoon and I'm helping Dad with our outside stuff on Saturday. Now's our only chance."

"Today's the biggest shopping day of the year," Claire told Alex. "Are you certain you want to brave the crowd?"

Alex shrugged. "Like Jennie said, if we don't do it now, I don't know when we will."

"I suppose not." Although Claire wanted to join the rest of the holiday bargain-hunters as much as she wanted a migraine, she knew when she'd lost the fight. "If you'll give me a few minutes to find Joshua's coat, we'll go."

"Great." Alex seemed pleased.

She motioned toward her sofa. "Make yourself comfortable. We'll be back shortly."

Alex thought about waiting in the foyer where they were, but curiosity got the better of him. He wanted to see Claire in her element, to catch a glimpse of the woman behind the uniform. Without further urging, he accepted her invitation and sat on an overstuffed chair.

The room possessed the same restful quality he associated with Claire. It wasn't cluttered with furnishings, but what she owned was good quality. A soft fleece blanket was tossed over the back of an overstuffed chair and a pile of oversized pillows suggested a lot of time spent on the floor.

The fireplace was actually a natural gas heater, which was great considering how one could create the mood of a cozy fire without the mess of ashes or the problem of finding wood.

"Hey, Dad," Jennie whispered.

Alec smiled at her. "What?"

"She doesn't have hardly any Christmas stuff set out."

He'd noticed. A strand of lights lined the mantel and a small stocking with Joshua's name sewn in script hung from a peg set off to one side. A tiny tree that was best described as a twig stood on an end table in the corner.

"Poor Joshua," Jennie mourned.

"Why do you say that?"

"He needs more than this." She waved her arms.

He thought so, too, but he wasn't making the decisions. "Claire obviously doesn't agree."

"Can we invite them over to our house so Joshua can see our tree when it's finished?"

Alec managed to hide his surprise. His daughter, who'd made a habit of treating his rare dates with cool disdain, had just suggested that he bring another woman into their home. From day one he'd worked hard to make up for his ex-wife's rejection of their daughter, but Jennie's reluctance to meet the few women he'd taken out over the years had made him equally reluctant to press the issue.

Maybe times were changing. Maybe Claire had struck a chord with Jennie that no one else had. He could hope. His attraction to Claire was making it harder and harder to ignore his own need for adult feminine companionship.

"What a great idea," he said. "We'll do it."

She grinned. "It'll be so exciting to see his face."

In the next instant he heard the distinct patter of small running feet and Claire calling Joshua's name.

He ran into the room all giggles with his dark blue coat zipped to his neck, his stocking cap tied under his chin and his mittens hanging from his sleeves. He headed straight for the sofa and hurled himself into Alex's lap. Then, as if surprised to see this strange person in his place on the sofa, he rose on his knees to stare at Alex.

Alex placed a hand on Joshua's back to keep him from tumbling over backward as he shifted position to move the youngster's knee out of his groin. It had been a while since Jennie had been this small and Alex was reminded of how fun—and demanding—a child this age was.

"Off," Joshua demanded, tugging on his cap.

Claire arrived just then, her coat unbuttoned. "Oh, Joshua." Her tone sounded exasperated. "I'm sorry, Alex. He's started this game of running away and jumping on the sofa before we leave."

"I don't mind," he said, eyeing the little boy who stared at him, then at Jennie, with unabashed interest. "Next time I'll wear a suit of armor."

Her gaze traveled to his lap and a becoming pink hue spread across her cheekbones. "I'm so sorry."

"I'm OK," he assured her.

"As for you, young man," she told Joshua firmly, "climb down and come here."

Once again, he pulled on the knit cap. "Off."

"Leave your hat on," she said. "We're going bye-bye."

"Bye-bye?"

Alex smiled at the youngster and noticed how the shape of his nose and mouth were carbon copies of Claire's. "Are you ready to go?" he asked.

Joshua bobbed his head. "Go."

"We'd better put on your mittens first," Alex said, reaching for the one dangling on the right.

Now co-operative, Joshua held out his hand. "Mitt."

While Alex slipped it over Joshua's hand, Claire did the same with the left. It was a thoroughly domesticated scene, Alex thought, inhaling Claire's berry scent as she bent over the two of them. Sadly, he couldn't remember one similar when Jennie had been little. Donna had left their lives before Jennie's first winter and on her rare visits after that, she'd been happy to let Alex handle all the parenting.

"OK, Buster Brown," she said as she held out her hands. "Come here."

Joshua slid off Alex's lap, unconcerned about which body part his small feet used as leverage. Instead of going to Claire, he stood by Jennie. "Play."

Jennie grinned at him. "When we come back."

"Come back." Joshua nodded as if apparently satisfied by her promise. He held out his hand as if he expected her to take it and she did.

"He's a friendly fellow," Alex said as he brought up the rear on their way to the front door.

"He doesn't know a stranger," Claire said. "I suppose it's because he's used to going to a babysitter's. He loves being with the older kids, like Jennie."

Outside, she gathered Joshua in her arms and started down the steps toward the detached garage.

"We'll take my vehicle," he said, motioning to the bronze Oldsmobile Bravada parked at the curb.

"He needs a car seat," she said.

"It's built in," he told her. "I'll have it ready in a minute." Then, because they were approaching a patch of ice on the sidewalk, he grabbed Claire's arm. "Be careful," he cautioned.

"Thanks."

Even after they'd navigated the icy spot, he found himself unwilling to let go. All he could think about was how he could do this again, but without the benefit of a coat between them.

A mental picture of her wearing the slinky party gowns common to the clinic Christmas party filled his mind's eye. He didn't need a glittery formal to appreciate her feminine attributes, but he ached with a desire to see her in something other than a uniform or a sweatshirt. Still, he couldn't complain too loudly. Her snug jeans revealed a shapelier form than he'd first imagined. When Joshua had pulled on her shirt and unveiled her creamy shoulder, a sweet shudder of desire flashed through him.

He'd definitely been alone for too long.

Ten minutes later, everyone was buckled in and they were headed to the local discount store, which sold everything from hardware to housewares.

As Claire had warned and he'd expected, the parking lot was filled to capacity.

"I wonder if anyone's at home," she joked.

"Probably not." He pulled into an empty stall at the far end of the property. "I'm afraid we can't park any closer."

"I don't mind walking," she said.

As Alex ushered their group toward the building, he noticed the wet pavement. Before he could determine if it was simply wet or a condition of black ice, Claire lost her footing. Without thinking, he hauled her up against him and held her securely. For a few seconds he couldn't breathe because the caress of her warm breath against his chin was quite arousing.

"Oh, my." Her voice came out in breathless gasps. "I'd better pay attention to where I'm going."

He found it difficult, if not impossible to release her. "I'll carry Josh."

She smiled as she shook her head. "I can manage."

"I'm sure you can," he said blandly, "but I'd rather not run the risk of broken bones." He let go, wondering if she noticed his reluctance, but retained his grip on one arm. "Jennie, hold my hand. We'll take it nice and easy."

The air was cold and by the time they reached the safety of the store's entrance, Joshua's and Jennie's cheeks were rosy.

Alex commandeered the last available cart and waited patiently for Claire to fit Joshua in the child's seat and remove his stocking cap. Alex's gaze followed her long fingers as they stroked Josh's static-charged wisps of hair and realized his ache was simply a craving for her touch.

This was definitely a sad state of affairs.

"Off to the fabric," Claire said as she smiled at his daughter.

Her comment was a trumpet call to reality. "I'll occupy Josh while you girls do your thing," he said.

An uncertain look crossed Claire's face as she unzipped her hip-length parka. "Are you sure?"

"We'll be within yelling distance," he promised.

Claire and Jennie threaded a path through the shopping-crowd obstacle course. Intent on keeping up with them for Josh's peace of mind, he trained his gaze on Claire and received an unexpected bonus in the process.

He had the nicest view of her trim behind and enjoyed every inch of it. The gentle sway of her hips parched his mouth and made swallowing difficult.

"You have a very pretty mommy," he murmured to Joshua.

Joshua grinned and wiggled his entire body. "Go."

"I'm going."

Claire glanced over her shoulder a few times, prepared to step in if Joshua didn't co-operate with the new person in his life, but it soon became obvious how unfounded her worries were. Joshua was listening to Alex in rapt wonder, as if Alex's deeper, tenor tone was far more interesting than the women's and children's voices he normally heard.

With luck, they'd leave the store long before Joshua decided he was hungry, although she carried a small container of bite-sized snacks in her oversized purse for emergencies.

"First stop, the patterns," Claire said cheerfully.

With the design and yardage information in hand, they hunted through the stacks of fabric for the right material until they found a bolt of white cotton flannel that was used for infant sleepwear. It was soft and would hang in graceful folds, which seemed appropriate for her character.

"Too bad I have to be a white angel," Jennie mourned as she fingered a gauzy gold piece in the clearance bin.

"We could use that for the wings," Claire said, "or are you supposed to wear them?"

"Mrs Vincent didn't say."

"Every angel needs a set. We'll take it."

Jennie's face lit up. "Really? But what if I'm the only kid who's got 'em?"

"Then you'll be extra-special, like Gabriel." Claire glanced at Alex and Joshua and smiled as her serious-minded boss rubbed the pieces of faux fur against her son's face, eliciting a childish giggle.

She'd been right. Alex *was* different when he was away from the practice, and yet he wasn't. The qualities that made him a good physician showed through in the man, but it was more likely a case of his inherent good qualities turning him into a highly recommended and sought-after physician.

"What are you looking at?"

"Just checking on Joshua," she answered as she turned

her attention back to fabric. "I think we should add some gold trim to match your gold wings."

"Wow. I'm going to be the most spectacular angel there."

"I wouldn't be surprised if you are."

Jennie fingered a roll of sheer blue ribbon liberally dotted with flecks of silver and silver snowflakes. "Isn't this pretty?"

"Yes, it is, but I don't think it would look right on your costume," Claire said gently, hoping the youngster wouldn't want to add it.

"Oh, I wasn't thinking about my outfit. Wouldn't it look nice on our snowflake and icicle tree?"

"Hmmm, let's see." Claire unrolled a length of the ribbon. "You know, this might be just the thing we needed. We could drape it on the branches or turn it into bows."

"And no one else would have anything like it," Jennie exclaimed. "Our tree would be one of a kind."

"We'll buy it," Claire decided.

In the end, they took two entire rolls. "Because we aren't sure of how much we'll need," Claire explained to Alex. "If the cost is over our limit, though, we'll—"

"We're not over budget," he assured her. "We could even afford to buy a few more frills. Not many. Just a few."

His warning to his daughter came through quite plainly. "This is all we need, right, Jennie?"

The little girl beamed. "Right."

Checkout lines were long, and between Joshua's fast-approaching lunchtime and boredom with sitting in the cart, he fussed.

"I think he's hungry," Jennie said.

"He is." Claire pulled out her plastic snack container. Sensing that Jennie was growing bored with the wait, she gave her a job. "Would you give him a few of these at a time?"

Jennie eagerly took over.

Alex leaned closer. "You must have been a Girl Scout."

"No, why?"

He motioned to the snack. "You're prepared."

Claire laughed. "Oh, no. I learned that the hard way."

Finally, it was their turn. Claire took Jennie and Joshua to look at the display of outdoor Christmas decorations near the front of the store while Alex paid for their purchases. Before the three of them reached the inner set of plate-glass windows, she heard a loud crash, and then everything seemed to happen at once. A whoosh of cold air, the crunch of glass, the groan of twisting metal, and screams that seemed to echo.

Instinctively, Claire closed her eyes and bent her head to protect her face from flying debris, at the same time turning to shield the children. Something hit her left shoulder so hard that the force drove her feet out from under her.

She was too stunned to imagine or figure out what had happened. She only knew that her shoulder hurt and her ears rang from the cries for help, but those things faded into the background as one thought ran through her mind without stopping.

Were Joshua and Jennie safe?

CHAPTER FIVE

ALEX had never known fear like he did at that moment. Seeing Claire and the children in the middle of such a horrifying scene was the stuff of nightmares.

And it had happened before his eyes.

Because he'd kept his gaze intent on the last spot where he'd seen Claire, he'd found her first and with relatively little difficulty. An elderly gentleman lay across her legs, a mangled shopping cart next to her. Fortunately, they were on the edge of the disaster, rather than in the thick of things. He didn't want to think about what he'd find there.

"Claire," he urged hoarsely, running his hands over her head to check for injuries. "Can you hear me?"

She opened her eyes and he was relieved to see a flash of recognition. "Alex?"

"I need to move you where it's safe."

"You have to look for the children. They were next to me when it happened and now they're not. You have to find them."

"Don't panic. I will," he promised gently, before he stood up and raised his voice. "Everyone, just lie still. We'll get you out, but give us time."

The store manager obviously heard the authority in Alex's voice, because he joined him. "I've called 911."

"Keep everyone away from here," he told the thirtyish manager. "As soon as we pull people free, we'll need an area set aside for the paramedics to work." Then, because the man clearly seemed uncertain about taking orders from him, he added, "I'm a doctor. Find plenty of blankets and have someone check the driver of that car."

A sky blue four-door Plymouth Neon was now part of the storefront window, its sole occupant slumped over the steering-wheel.

With that information, the manager—John Peel, according to his ID tag—didn't hesitate. He immediately began organizing his employees to do as Alex had asked.

Several began tossing around pieces of the destroyed wall and scattered merchandise, but Alex stopped them. "Don't lift anything if it will cause another piece to fall," he cautioned his impromptu but able-bodied rescue crew. "We don't want these folks worse off than they are. If you aren't sure if you can move someone, then don't. The ambulances and fire department will be here shortly."

The three men nodded, and returned to their task with more cautious enthusiasm.

Alex glanced behind Claire and saw Jennie's familiar red coat and Joshua's little blue parka lying amidst the mess, a few feet away. Unfortunately, to get to them he had to move Claire, and to move her he had to move the fellow who'd pinned her to the ground.

"Can you see the kids?" she asked.

"Yes," he said. "But we have to play pick-up sticks first. I can't reach them otherwise." He moved to check the elderly gentleman who had started to groan.

"Hurry," she mumbled.

As if he needed urging. He noticed the man had several deep cuts to his face from the flying glass and he began feeling for broken bones. Fortunately, he found none, or at least none that were obvious.

"How are you doing?" he asked the fellow.

The man touched his bleeding face. "Like I got hit by a freight train. What happened?"

"A car crashed into the store."

"No kidding?"

"No kidding," Alex said. "Can you move?"

He gingerly moved his legs. "Yeah. My foot's stuck on something, though."

Alex shifted the pile of crushed popcorn tins lying across his lower body until he saw the problem. The shelf that had held the merchandise had buckled and was resting at a drunken angle on the man's foot. He lifted the shelf without earning a hernia for his efforts, and the elderly fellow slid his leg free. A minute later, Alex had placed him in the care of a woman employee who immediately flung a blanket around his shoulders and led him to the now-deserted checkout area.

"Your turn," he told Claire as he helped her to her feet. The distant wail of sirens had never sounded so good. "The cavalry is coming."

"Thank goodness." Her next breath was a groan and she sagged in his arms.

"What's wrong?"

"Shoulder," she gasped. "But don't worry about it now. Get Joshua and Jennie."

Someone else had taken his place, so by the time he returned to the spot where he'd extricated Claire, Jennie was being freed from the broken aisle display of canned soda.

"Daddy," she exclaimed as she ran into his arms.

He ran his hands over her head, taking in the scratches on her face which had already stopped bleeding. "Are you OK?"

She nodded. "But my coat is ripped."

The fabric showed long gashes and he was glad that this was coat and sweater weather. Ripped clothing was easier and less messy to repair than ripped skin.

"Don't worry about it," he told her. "We'll either fix it or buy a new one. Wait with Claire while I look at Joshua."

"OK."

The little boy lay motionless in a veritable sea of soda

cans and plastic bottles. A deep gash across his forehead and a goose egg at the back of his head where he'd obviously hit the floor told the tale.

"Hi, Alex. Fancy seeing you here." Alex's neighbor, twenty-five-year-old Morey Keaton, knelt beside him and opened his kit of supplies. Not only was he a paramedic for the city, but his wife was Alex's patient and they were now proud parents of a two-month-old daughter. Alex had let Morey catch young Brianna as she'd been born and the light in Morey's eyes hadn't dimmed from the experience yet.

"Yeah. Are you coming on duty or going off?"

"I came on this morning," Morey told him as he ripped open a package of gauze and held it out to Alex. "Do you need anything else?"

"Hold that on his head for a minute." While the paramedic obeyed, Alex helped himself to latex gloves. "How about a penlight?"

Morey reached into his left shirt pocket and handed it over. "I hope this kid's parents aren't under that mess." He inclined his head in the direction of the car's front fender.

"We already got her out. She's waiting on aisle five."

Alex quickly checked Joshua's pupils and was pleased to see them responsive to light. He peeked under the pressure pad and examined the edges of Joshua's gash. "He's going to need stitches."

Joshua's eyelids fluttered until his eyes opened. At first he stared blankly at Alex, but then he began to cry.

"It's OK, Josh," Alex soothed the little boy, who was both hurt and scared. "You're going to be fine."

"Do you want a neck brace?" Keaton asked.

"Yeah. Let's play it safe."

"We'll transport him and his mom together," Morey said.

"Good idea. Can you take Jennie, too? Just so she's out

of the way? I'm going to stay for a little longer. Someone might need a doctor."

Two Emergency Services people waved in their direction. "Keaton. Over here."

Morey motioned to a fireman who brought a stretcher. "Ship him out a.s.a.p."

Alex went over to Claire, who'd struggled to her feet. "What's wrong with Joshua?" she asked, clearly worried and frightened.

"He's had a bad bump to his head and was unconscious for a few minutes," Alex told her. "They're taking him in for a CT scan."

"Oh, God. I need to go with him." Her voice rose.

"Of course," Alex said, "but don't panic. He's awake, but he probably has a huge headache." He glanced in Morey's direction in time to see him wave her forward. "I'll meet the three of you at the hospital so don't worry."

Claire nodded and she grabbed Jennie's hand. Alex hoped she'd heard everything he'd said, but if not, he knew where to find her. Joshua would require close observation and nothing would draw her from his side.

Then, because it seemed like the thing to draw her out of her shock, he planted a firm, hard kiss on her lips. "I'll see you later."

He'd expected to surprise her by his impulsive action, but her only reaction was a slight widening of her eyes.

"Ma'am. We need to go," a paramedic said.

Without hesitation, she hurried after the stretcher-bearing men as Jennie waved goodbye to him over her shoulder.

Alex wondered if Claire would ever remember his brief kiss, but it didn't matter if she forgot. Now that he'd stolen a sample, nothing would stop him from going after a full meal.

*   *   *

Claire sat next to Joshua's hospital crib and stroked his small hand. After three hours, blood tests, brain scans and X-rays, the diagnosis had been plain and, according to the ER physician, straightforward.

Mild concussion.

Yet she couldn't quite believe it. He lay too quietly for her peace of mind—normally, he was quite active even while he slept—but she didn't want him fussy either, because she couldn't hold him. Although she knew the signs and the treatment, she analyzed his every move and tried to second-guess every complication she'd ever studied, read about or seen.

What if the ER doctor had missed something?

Just considering that thought caused a fresh wave of nausea.

The door opened soundlessly and she glanced up to see Alex. Strong, confident, rock-solid Alex. Instant relief swept over her.

He was Joshua's doctor and although she doubted if she'd truly believe Joshua was fine until he acted his usual rambunctious self, she wanted Alex's assurances.

He smiled at her as he walked in, his glance sweeping briefly to Jennie who lay asleep on the empty bed.

"How is he?" he asked, his low voice barely above a whisper.

"Resting. Did you look at his test results?"

"Right before I came in. He'll be running around tomorrow as if nothing had happened."

She nibbled on her lip to keep her mouth from trembling. "Do you think so?"

"Sure. He has a hard head." He smiled. "How are you?"

Claire touched her shoulder. "Fine. Bruised, but unbroken. Dr Simmons wants me to wear a sling for a few days."

"And Jennie?"

"A few scratches, a few bumps. For the record, I don't

think I could have managed without her,'' Claire said fervently. "She entertained Joshua while I was being looked after and even when I wasn't, she played with him." She grinned. "Joshua isn't going to be satisfied with me as his only playmate any more."

"Seems like sewing and babysitting are fair exchanges," he said.

"How are things at the Super-Mart? Was anyone hurt badly?"

"The kid driving had some burns from the air bag and a couple of shoppers had broken bones. We admitted a few—one was bleeding internally when the doorframe snapped and hit his abdomen, but the last I heard, he was doing OK in surgery. One had a skull fracture and we airlifted him to a neuro unit. Everyone else had minor cuts and bruises."

"I'm glad. Did the police figure out what happened?"

"Apparently the teenage girl behind the wheel was reaching for her cellphone when she hit that icy patch in front of the store."

Claire remembered that spot well. Alex hadn't let go of her arm until they'd been well past it.

"The car fishtailed, she panicked, overcompensated and slid right through the plate-glass window. She's just lucky she didn't drive over a pedestrian."

Claire shuddered at the thought. "Did they close the store?"

He grinned as he shook his head. "And miss an opportunity to earn a buck? Hardly. When I left with the last injured person, they were already covering the hole with plastic. My guess is that once news leaks out, everyone in town will want to see the damage first hand."

"Probably."

"We missed lunch and now it's almost time for dinner. Why don't we grab a bite from the cafeteria?"

"I couldn't."

"A cup of coffee."

She pointed to the three empty styrofoam cups on the bedside table. "If I drink any more caffeine, I'll be like the television Energizer Bunny."

"OK, but grab your coat. I'll run you home."

The idea was unthinkable. "I can't leave."

"Not even to freshen up?"

"The nurse said I could use the shower here."

"What about clothes?"

"Nora will bring what I need. She has my spare key. How long do you think he'll have to stay?" Claire tensed. Normally they kept a patient in overnight for observation, but if Alex suggested a longer time, she'd know something was wrong—something they weren't telling her.

"If he has a good night, then I don't see why he can't leave in the morning," he said.

Unable to speak, she simply nodded.

Apparently awakened by the sound of their voices, Jennie sat up and rubbed her eyes. "Hi, Daddy."

He strode to her side. "Hi, honeybunch. Are you ready to go home?"

"Yeah. Claire bought crackers from the machine and the nurse brought Joshua a sandwich, but he wouldn't eat it, so I did. I'm still hungry, though."

He chuckled. "Then we'd better fix that, hadn't we?"

Jennie slid off the bed. "Is it too late to get our tree tonight?"

"Probably not."

"Yippee!" At both adults' "Shh", she covered her mouth with both hands and looked sheepish. "Sorry," she whispered. "But we *can* pick it out right now, can't we?"

"On our way home," he promised. "We'll leave the decorating until tomorrow."

Jennie nodded, then spoke to Claire. "Will you and Joshua come over and help us? He'd really like our twinkly lights and glittery stuff."

"I'll bet he would," Claire answered, surprised by Jennie's invitation and yet loath to accept, "but I doubt if he'll be in a happy mood."

"Once he sees it, he'll get happy," Jennie insisted. "You don't have a big tree, so this will be something new and exciting for him."

Once again, a twinge of guilt struck her. "I'm sure he'd be thrilled, but—"

"It's all part of celebrating Jesus being born," Jennie continued. "We'll have hot chocolate and Mrs Rowe has gingerbread cookies, and when we're all done we can go to your house and work on my costume."

Clearly, Jennie had planned everything, and Claire hated to burst the child's bubble. She looked at Alex and silently begged for help.

"I'm sure Claire and Joshua will come if they can," he said firmly, "and if Josh feels better in the morning."

"OK, but I know he'd enjoy himself if he was there. I was a kid once, too, you know."

Claire smiled at Jennie's grown-up tone. "Whatever we choose to do, thank you for the invitation. Have fun picking out your tree."

Jennie nodded and her eyes shone with anticipation. "We will."

Alex leaned closer to Claire. "I'll see you later."

He didn't explain if "later" meant this evening or tomorrow, but Claire didn't press him. As much as she hated for him to leave, he couldn't stay. He had his own family responsibilities just as she had hers.

"If you need me, call," he ordered.

"I don't have your number."

He glanced around the room, and then yanked a paper towel from the dispenser and scribbled on it. "Here," he said. "If you lose this, the nurses at the desk know how to reach me."

Lose those two sets of numbers? Not a chance. They were her lifeline, her security blanket.

"Thanks," she said instead.

Alex stood over her and lightly clasped her good shoulder. "He's going to be fine. Don't worry. Now, get some rest. Once Joshua starts feeling better, you won't have time to recuperate yourself." With that, he left the room as soundlessly as he'd appeared, leaving Claire with her thoughts, the faintest trace of his woodsy scent and his touch indelibly marked on her shoulder.

Had he truly kissed her this morning, or had she simply imagined it?

No, she hadn't dreamt it. Neither could she chalk it up to wishful thinking. Either of those options wouldn't account for the pressure she could feel on her lips if she closed her eyes.

He'd kissed her and—heaven help her—she wanted him to do it again. This time preferably when she could enjoy it to the fullest.

She exchanged her straight-backed chair for the recliner and, after pulling it close to the crib so Joshua would see her if he woke, she relaxed and listened to the sound of her son's soft, steady breathing.

He probably wouldn't notice if she went home for a quick shower and a change of clothes, but she simply couldn't tear herself away. She wouldn't tempt fate by leaving if Joshua couldn't. She wasn't taking any chances.

She dozed fitfully until the door opened once again. She opened her eyes and was surprised to see that the man who'd invaded her dreams had returned.

"I thought you'd be gone longer than five minutes," she teased.

He quirked one lazy eyebrow. "Five minutes? It's been three hours."

"Three hours? It can't be." She glanced at the window.

Darkness had replaced the sunshine she'd seen earlier through the slats of the mini-blinds.

"It's seven-thirty," he told her. "If you don't know what time it is, then I don't have to ask if you've eaten."

"I'm not hungry."

"Hmm." Before she could puzzle out what he meant by that, he went to the door and, after beckoning to someone, returned with Nancy Thompson, Joshua's pediatric nurse, in tow.

"Nancy will watch him while we dash down to the cafeteria," he said.

"I can't go."

"Yes, you can and you will."

"I'm not hungry."

"I am."

"Didn't you eat dinner with Jennie?"

"I dropped her off at my mother's. When I left, they were deciding on what type of pizza to order."

"You didn't need to come back," she began, grateful that he had.

"I always check on my favorite patient and his mother," he said. "Let's go so Nancy can do her job."

"But—"

Alex grabbed her hand and pulled her out of the easy chair. "Thirty minutes. No more, no less."

"I'll keep a close eye on him," Nancy promised.

Claire had already learned Nancy's credentials. She'd worked in pediatrics for ten years and in a PICU—or pediatric intensive care unit—for five years before that. In essence, she was placing Joshua in more capable hands than her own, but knowing that didn't make her leaving easier.

Alex ushered her to the door before she could dig in her heels. With one hand at her back, he guided her into the hallway.

"Nancy has plenty of other sick kids to watch," she

told him as he stopped in front of the elevator to push the "down" button.

"Nancy is doing what she's getting paid to do which, for the next thirty minutes, is looking after Josh," Alex said. "Now, take a deep breath and think about what you'd like to eat."

Hospital planners had located the cafeteria in the basement and as soon as they stepped out of the elevator, the aromas coaxed a growl out of her stomach.

"Help yourself to whatever you want," he told her as he steered her to the hot-food line.

Nothing sounded good so, because he was glowering at her, she requested a bowl of chicken-noodle soup.

Alex had been ready to load her tray himself until she'd finally made her selection. He thought she needed something more substantial, but she obviously hadn't regained her appetite after their harrowing experience.

Yet, as they sat in a quiet corner, Claire's face appeared far too white for his liking.

Guessing at the cause, he reached across the table to cover her hand with his. "Josh is going to be fine. Stop worrying."

"Easier said than done," she said wryly.

"Trust me. He'll be fine."

The spoon she'd placed in her bowl remained there as she stared at her soup with a fixed expression. "I know. It's just that…"

"What?"

She blinked, as if mentally pulling herself out of her trance, and waved her right hand. "It's nothing. Forget it."

"It isn't nothing," he insisted. "And I *won't* forget it."

"It's silly."

"If you're troubled, then it isn't silly."

She shrugged. "I'm so afraid of losing him."

"You won't."

"His father died at Christmas-time, you see. One day

we discovered he had a virulent form of cancer and within weeks he was gone. I couldn't bear it if I lost Joshua, too.''

That explained her dislike of the holiday, even though she'd tried to hide it.

"You won't lose him," he stated again. If he repeated it often enough, she might start to believe it.

"I know, but down in here..." she pressed on her breastbone "...I still worry."

"Would it make you feel better if I asked another doctor for a second opinion?"

She shook her head. "It's not that I don't trust your judgment. It's just that something unexpected could happen." Her attempt at laughter fell short. "I tell myself that I'm not jinxed when it comes to Christmas, that fate wouldn't be so unkind as to take two people away from me during this time, but the truth is, it could happen."

"And an asteroid could crash through the ceiling right now," he said.

"You're making fun of me."

"No. Never. I'm just trying to tell you that the odds are against it and you can't dwell on that one in a million chance."

"I know, but—"

"But nothing. It's easy to think the worst when you're tired, so as soon as you've had your soup, we're going back upstairs and you're going to bed."

"But Joshua—"

"Will probably sleep all night," he said. "And if he doesn't, we have nursing staff on duty to take care of his every need. Now, no arguments. How's the recliner?"

"Hard," she answered wryly.

"Typical," he said.

"Speaking from experience?"

"I spent many a night in recliners just like that one," he said as he dug into his mashed potatoes and gravy, pleased to see Claire doing the same with her soup. "The surgeon fixed Jennie's cleft lip a few weeks after she was born. One specialist wanted to wait until she was several months old and another wanted to repair it right away. I would have gone with his recommendation, but she developed an ear infection and we had to postpone.''

"Was her palate affected as well?"

He nodded. "Her soft palate but not the hard. The surgeon corrected that when she was about six months old.''

"She was rather young, wasn't she?"

"The timing is still controversial. They claim the earlier it's done, the better it is in terms of the child's speech and hearing. Others believe that if surgery is done too soon, the teeth buds can be damaged or normal facial bone growth will be affected. It was a tough decision.''

"But you opted for early treatment.''

"It seemed worth the risk. And…'' he let out a deep sigh ''…I thought it might help my wife bond with our baby.''

"She had a hard time coping?"

"To say the least. She refused to look at Jennie or hold her. As you know, these babies have special needs when it comes to feeding, and Donna simply refused to handle that aspect of her care.''

"I'm sorry,'' she said softly.

"I am, too. Donna was—is—a beautiful woman, and I thought that once the obvious had been corrected, she'd accept her daughter for the lovely baby she was. I was mistaken.''

"And you grew to resent her.''

"Hell, yes, I did,'' he exploded, before he tempered his tone. "Just because she'd been a model and was an airline attendant who'd worked her way into the first-class overseas flights, it didn't mean that she could ignore her daughter.''

"But she did.''

He nodded. "As soon as her gynecologist gave her a

clean bill of health, she returned to work. By the time Jennie was as normal as modern medicine could make her, Donna had decided to replace us. We divorced before Jennie's first birthday, which was probably a blessing in the long run.''

"So she never knew her mother?"

"Not in the true sense. Oh, Donna sends Jennie a birthday gift every year, but otherwise she's too busy with her new husband. He's a rich old geezer who can afford her collagen and botox whenever she wants them.''

"It's a shame that Jennie missed out on the mothering experience, but you've done a marvelous job with her," Claire said. "She's a delightful little girl."

"Thanks. She's pretty special in my books, too."

Claire pushed aside her nearly empty bowl. "I can't eat another bite. That was delicious."

He grinned. "What did I tell you?"

On their way to the elevator, Claire stopped in her tracks. "I forgot to ask. Did you find your tree? I suppose you chose the biggest on the lot."

Her smile and teasing tone made her sound more like her old self. "Not quite," he said ruefully. "Fortunately, we have eight-foot ceilings in our house, so I'm able to convince Jennie that a seven-foot pine will look perfect." He sobered. "She really wants you and Joshua to come over.''

She dropped her gaze and crossed her arms. "I know she does, but I wouldn't be very good company."

"You can't ignore Christmas forever," he said.

Her eyes reflected her indecision. "I'll think about it."

He stroked the back of her hand, enjoying the softness of her skin. "That's all I ask."

The return trip to Joshua's room went much more quickly than Alex would have liked, but he didn't feel right in taking the scenic route if it kept Claire from Joshua any longer than he'd promised. She hadn't dwelt on her worries and perhaps, when she walked in and found Joshua as healthy as she'd left him, she'd rest easier.

"Now, I want you to sleep," he told Claire as soon as they walked into Joshua's room. "If you don't, I'll prescribe a sleeping pill."

"I'll be fine. Honest."

"OK. I'll see you in the morning and I expect to see you bright-eyed and bushy-tailed."

She grinned. "I'll do my best."

Later, as Alex lay in his own bed, his arms folded underneath the back of his head, he reflected on how lucky Joshua was to have such a caring mother. It still rankled him at times when he thought of Donna's selfishness, but if she *had* remained in the picture, he wouldn't have the close relationship that he did with his daughter.

Now, if only he could work out a relationship with Claire. In the meantime, however, he intended to do what he could to help Jennie in her efforts to spread Christmas cheer to the Westin household.

CHAPTER SIX

"WHAT have you decided?" Alex asked as he drove Claire and Joshua home on Saturday morning.

Claire had been waiting for his inevitable question. After stewing over the subject at odd times throughout the night, she still had a hard time answering.

What *had* she decided about Jennie's and Alex's invitation?

She had one reason to refuse and a dozen to accept... Joshua would enjoy the outing. Jennie would be thrilled and she herself would spend a pleasant afternoon with Alex.

If she didn't go, what else would she do? The few presents she'd purchased for Joshua and Nora's family were wrapped and ready for delivery. She didn't send out Christmas cards and had ordered holiday cookies instead of baking her own. She hadn't started Jennie's costume but, until they either found the fabric they'd bought or purchased more, she had no other commitments. That left curling up with a good book and drinking hot chocolate while Joshua napped.

What a choice. Spend the afternoon reading or being with Alex and feeling her toes tingle.

"Can't make up your mind?" he teased.

She managed a smile. "It shouldn't be a tough choice, but it is."

"In case you want my professional opinion, Josh probably won't suffer any ill effects if he spends a few hours away from home. It might be good for him. And for you."

"Is that your holiday prescription, Doctor?"

"One of them," he said.

"And the others are?" Claire looked at him expectantly, taking in the strong lines of his chin.

"I'll save those for another day," he said. "I'd hate to overdose you on holiday spirit."

She chuckled before her good mood dimmed. She'd feel guilty if she prevented Joshua from experiencing something that so many other children took for granted, but she'd feel equally as guilty if she went in search of a good time.

It was simply a matter of which choice carried the most condemnation.

"I think we'd better stay at home," she finally said.

Claire expected Alex to argue, but he simply said, "Jennie will be disappointed."

"I know, and I'm sorry. Tell her…" Her mind raced to think of a suitable consolation prize. "Tell her we'll drive by this evening to look at it."

"She's going to want to go back to the clinic," he reminded her. "We have to finish there, too."

"What about tomorrow?" Claire asked.

"Cutting our time frame a little close, aren't we? It would be simpler to go this evening and get it over with. Unless you prefer to have unfinished projects hanging over your head."

"I don't, but surely you planned something more interesting on a Saturday night?" *Like a date,* she wanted to add, but didn't.

The twinkle in his eye suggested that he'd read her mind. "Sorry to disappoint you, but I didn't."

"If you truly don't have other plans then, yes, we'll go to the office." Joshua would get a small taste of the joys associated with Christmas when they added the final touches to their snowflake tree. She'd reserve tomorrow to sew Jennie's costume.

"OK," she said. "This evening it is."

A few minutes later Alex parked his vehicle and helped

her into the house. Joshua immediately tore off his stocking cap and headed for his pile of toys in the living room. Several minutes later, she heard a familiar "beep, beep".

Alex grinned. "He sounds pretty normal to me."

"Yeah. Thank goodness."

"If you should change your mind about helping with our project at home, drop by," he told her. "Jennie wants to start around noon."

She didn't know what to say, so she simply nodded.

He turned to leave, then stopped. "I understand your reasons to avoid Christmas, but I don't have to like them," he said. "You can't run and hide forever."

Before she could answer, he was already halfway to his car. Claire watched him slide inside and drive away, his words still ringing in her ears.

"I'm not running," she said to the empty foyer. "Or hiding."

She stomped into the living room with righteous indignation, but as soon as she saw the pathetic tree and Joshua's stocking hanging forlornly from the mantel, the wind blew out of her sails.

Maybe she wasn't running away, but she wasn't walking forward either. She may have started over in other areas of her life, but in this one she was stuck in the same rut.

Joshua ran toward her and her personal dilemma took a back seat. "Mama. Dink."

"Drink," she said, instinctively correcting his pronunciation.

He bobbed his head as he grabbed her hand. "Dwink," he repeated. "Joo."

"OK, young man. I'll pour juice for you."

While he drank his cup of apple juice, Claire began fixing their lunch. Joshua hadn't eaten his breakfast in the hospital and because it was nearly eleven-thirty, she knew he'd be hungry soon. After he'd quenched his thirst, he sat in front of her cupboard and pulled out his favorite pots and pans.

Absent-mindedly, she watched the macaroni boil and reflected on her situation. Why should she conform to everyone's expectations about the holiday? Just because she didn't feel the need to go overboard like everyone else, it didn't mean that she was hiding.

Aren't you? her conscience persisted.

Before she could think about her answer, Joshua tugged on her pant leg. "Eat?"

She carefully, cautiously lifted him up and held him on one hip as she kissed his temple. "Just a few more minutes. Can you put your dishes away?"

He nodded. "Down."

Ten minutes later, she'd strapped him into his high chair and placed a plate of macaroni and cheese in front of him. It didn't take long before he was wearing as much of his dinner as he'd spooned into his mouth. By the time he started chasing macaroni across his high-chair tray with one finger, she knew he'd eaten enough.

"OK, son. You're just playing. Let's wash your face."

"Play?" he asked.

"For a little while," she said as she scrubbed his cheeks with a wet cloth.

"'Ennie?" he asked.

"Jennie isn't here," she answered, although her thoughts immediately drifted in Alex's direction. Her imagination pictured him moving boxes of Christmas decorations out of storage and Jennie enthusiastically opening each one. The room was probably a mess, with boxes and tissue paper all over the floor. Knowing Jennie, she was probably in seventh heaven.

"Toys," Joshua demanded.

"Yes, sir," she said, then gingerly lowered him out of his chair. "You may play with your toys."

While he scampered into the living room, presumably

to his toy corner, Claire washed their few dishes. Her imagination took her back to Alex's house. Would he pop in a CD of carols and sing along with Jennie?

She listened with her mother's ear and heard Joshua babbling to himself in their otherwise quiet house. At one time she would have played everything from Bing Crosby's holiday tunes to her collection of symphony Christmas music, but now she didn't even know where she'd stored those discs.

Alex's voice echoed in her head. *You can't run and hide forever.*

Before she could argue with herself, Joshua reappeared. "Mama. Watch me. Pease."

With a request like that, she couldn't refuse. She followed him into the living room and leaned against the doorframe, content to observe his driving skills as he rolled his trucks over the rug that pictured a town. Buildings of all kinds—a park and playground, a school and various stores—lined the winding streets and Joshua happily drove his vehicles with little regard for stop signs or pedestrians. Every now and then he took a short cut through buildings, trees and even a fire hydrant to reach whatever destination struck his fancy.

With his attention occupied, Claire tried to choose a book from her collection, but none of the titles appealed. Cover art went unnoticed because she saw Alex and Jennie stringing lights and hanging ornaments in her mind's eye.

Suddenly, her house seemed too lonely and far too quiet. She wanted—*needed*—to be in a room full of noise and laughter, watching the awe on Jennie's face appear on Joshua's.

It seemed a crime to deprive him of one of the season's joys.

She replaced the book on the shelf and stiffened her spine. "I'm doing this for our son, Ray," she whispered. "I hope you understand."

Before she could talk herself out of her decision, she said, "Come, Joshua. Let's find your coat so we can go bye-bye."

He immediately stood at hearing his favorite word. "Bye-bye?"

"Yes," she answered. "We're going to visit some very special people."

"You told Claire that she could come and help us with our tree, didn't you, Daddy?" Jennie demanded as she plugged in the string of lights to check the little bulbs after eleven months of storage.

"Yes, kiddo. I did."

"And you told her that I really, really, *really* wanted her here?"

"Yes, Jen. Claire knows. She agreed to stop by this evening and check out our work before we go to the clinic, so no pouting."

"But, Daddy, you're a *doctor*. When you say stuff, people are supposed to listen."

Alex chuckled at his daughter's idea. "They do if I give medical advice. In situations away from the hospital or clinic, it's their choice whether to listen or not."

"I do what you tell me," she reminded him.

"Because I'm the parent. Claire is a friend and she can decide what she wants to do in her spare time."

"You still should have told her that she *had* to come this afternoon," she mumbled.

"She'll come if she can," he said. "In the meantime, we'd better work on our tree or when she does stop by, she won't have anything to see."

"I still think Joshua needs a tree of his very own," Jennie insisted. "Couldn't we buy one for him? It wouldn't have to be big like ours. We could find something his size."

Alex intended to veto his daughter's suggestion, but the

more he thought about it, the more he liked it. Claire might refuse their gift, but if it was intended for Josh, he was reasonably certain she wouldn't.

On the other hand, if she did, he didn't want Jennie to walk away with crushed feelings. "I'll agree on two conditions."

Jennie bounded to her feet and jumped up and down in excitement. "What?"

"Claire might not appreciate us bringing a tree without her approval."

Jennie nodded. "You mean she might get mad."

"Exactly. If she refuses it, don't be upset."

"I promise I won't, but she won't turn it down."

Alex didn't have as much faith as his daughter, but nothing ventured was nothing gained. "She might."

Jennie shrugged, unconcerned. "If she does, we'll put it in our kitchen. Mrs Rowe won't care if we have two trees at our house, will she?"

He smiled at her. "No."

"What's the second condition?"

"I'll do the talking."

Her head bobbed. "Deal."

"Now, if we're going to accomplish this today, we'd better get busy."

They rushed to the closest lot selling Christmas trees, chose a four-foot tree that Jennie deemed was Joshua-sized, stuffed it in the back of his car and drove toward Claire's house.

Although Jennie was thrilled by what she termed "their secret mission", Alex hoped Claire would still speak to him when this was over. After his parting shot, she'd probably think he'd purposely planned to drag her out of her comfort zone. He hadn't, but he wasn't about to let the golden opportunity of Jennie's suggestion pass by.

Alex parked in Claire's driveway, fully expecting her to notice their arrival and race out of her house before they made it to the door. His luck held. As far as he could tell, not even a curtain had stirred.

Jennie carried the small bag containing an extra fifty-foot strand of lights while he hauled the tree onto the porch. After placing it away from the door and windows, out of sight, he whispered, "Don't forget. Let me—"

"I know. You'll do the talking."

Squaring his shoulders, he signaled Jennie to ring the doorbell.

Almost instantly the door opened and Claire stood before him, her coat on. Josh stood at her side, also dressed to go out in the cold.

"Hi, Nor—" She stopped in the middle of Nora's name, clearly surprised to see Alex.

"Hi," he said. "Have we caught you at a bad time?"

"No. Not at all. I thought you were Nora. I must say," she said, as a welcoming smile appeared on her face, "this is quite a treat. I'd pictured you both at home, hard at work."

She'd been thinking of them. A good sign, in Alex's opinion.

"We were," Jennie broke in, "but it didn't seem right for Joshua to miss out on the fun. We brought something special for him."

Alex cleared his throat and sent her a pointed look. She looked sheepish, but didn't say another word.

"Oh. That was nice of you." Claire stepped aside, snatching Joshua out of the way at the same time. "Please, come in."

"If you're leaving, we wouldn't want you to be late because of us," Alex mentioned.

A pink tinge crawled across her face. "Actually, we were on our way to your house."

"Well, well," he said in his most satisfied tone. "I'm sorry I spoilt my own surprise."

"I decided to do it for Joshua."

"Good. Then you won't be angry when you see what we've brought."

Alex reached for the small Christmas pine and gave it one last shake to dislodge the loose needles before he held it in front of the door for Claire to see.

Her jaw dropped. She tried to speak and couldn't, until at last an "Oh, my" came out of her mouth.

"Awesome, isn't it?" he asked.

"I already have a tree."

"Not like this one."

"You shouldn't have."

Her own words became his defense. "We did it for Joshua."

"It was my idea," Jennie piped up.

"How nice." Claire wasn't smiling. "You shouldn't have," she said again. "You *really* shouldn't have."

Alex knew he'd have to be his most persuasive. He'd won debate awards in high school, so he could surely convince Claire to accept one small gift. OK, it wasn't so small, but it was a gift.

"But we did, so may we come in?"

As he'd anticipated, her manners were too well ingrained to keep them standing in the cold. She stepped aside and, pressing his momentary advantage, he carried the tree into the foyer.

"Daddy said you might be upset, but you're not, are you?" Jennie peered at her. "If you are, please, don't get mad at him. This was my idea."

"I see." Claire regarded him with apparent suspicion.

Alex shrugged his shoulders and flashed his most brilliant smile. "It was," he said. "In fact, I wish I'd thought of it."

"Look, Alex—" she began.

"Jennie?" He turned to his daughter. "Why don't you and Josh go into the other room while Claire and I discuss this?"

Without further urging, she grabbed Joshua's hand. "Let's play."

Joshua didn't require a second invitation and the two disappeared into the living room.

"All right, Alex. What are you doing?"

"I'm delivering a Christmas tree at my daughter's request."

"You know how I feel about...this." She motioned to the pine.

"Yes, but did you or did you not say that you were on your way to my place?"

"That's different," she snapped.

It struck him how beautiful she was when she was angry. The fire in her eyes was a perfect match to the fiery highlights in her hair. "Not really," he said.

"It is. Really."

"You were going to let Josh help us decorate ours. Can't you allow him to enjoy his own? One that he can look at every day, all day, whenever he wants to?" he wheedled.

Her shoulders slumped and moisture brimmed in her eyes, effectively dousing the fire he'd seen before. Anger he could handle, but not tears.

Remorse filled him and he stepped forward to wrap his arms around her. "I'm sorry. We only wanted to bring you and Josh a piece of Christmas. I didn't intend to push so hard or upset you."

She buried her face in his coat and nodded. He assumed she'd accepted his apology.

He stood there for a minute, inhaling the scent of her hair and enjoying the way she felt in his arms with her head tucked under his chin.

Several weeks ago, his mother had asked what he wanted for Christmas, but he hadn't known at the time. Now, although she couldn't possibly fulfill his heart's desire, he knew what he wanted as well as he knew his own name.

Claire. He wanted Claire.

As much as he hated to admit that her tears were his fault, he was fighting for this small victory. The battle wasn't about Joshua, although he played a key role. It was about him and his need to know that Claire was completely free to love again. She'd taken several big steps to move on with her life—relocating to Pleasant Valley had been one—but until she worked through her aversion to this winter holiday, her first husband would always have an unrelenting grip on her.

Perhaps he wouldn't care about that state of affairs if he was only interested in an occasional evening with her. The fact was, he wanted to be Claire's *second* husband, and he wanted to enjoy every season of the year with her, including Christmas.

He continued to hold her, gradually realizing that winning the war meant more than winning this particular skirmish. If he had to retreat today, then he would.

"If you don't want the tree, I'll get rid of it."

She raised her head off his coat and avoided his gaze as she backed out of his embrace. With shaky fingers, she wiped her cheeks. "No. It's here and we'll—I'll—make the best of it."

He reached out and brushed away a tear lingering in the corner of her eye. "Good girl. And speaking of being good, where's your sling?"

"It was in my way. I couldn't do anything while I wore it."

"That's the idea."

"I know, but for me it's not practical. Like the tree."

"It's not supposed to be practical. It's supposed to be fun. A break in the monotony."

"Maybe so, but I still can't believe you bought it for us."

"I'm a little surprised myself," he admitted. "Now that you've decided to keep our gift, where would you like it?"

The mischief appearing in her eyes warned him that she'd recovered from her shock and had a specific location in mind—an anatomically impossible location.

"The living room, dining room or kitchen?" he added.

"The living room. We'll move the table out of the corner and set the tree there."

He was quick to relocate furniture to her instructions. While she laid plastic on the floor to protect the carpeting, he carried in the pine, placed it in its temporary place of honor, then stepped back for the view.

A bare spot faced him, so he repositioned the evergreen. "What a perfect place for a Christmas tree," he said.

"Do you like our surprise?" Jennie asked Claire.

"It was thoughtful of you," she answered. "Joshua will enjoy it, I'm sure."

Jennie leaned over and hugged the little boy. "This is so exciting," she chattered to him. "You have a real, live tree."

"I'll reimburse you for the cost," Claire murmured to Alex.

"This is Jennie's gift to Josh," he said firmly, feeling quite cheerful over how well the situation had turned out. "It was the runt of the litter, so to speak, and they gave us a good deal."

"I'm afraid it will stay rather bare," she said wryly. "Our ornaments are stored in the garage and I can't get to them without a lot of reshuffling."

He guessed they were stashed in a relatively inaccessible area, like the rafters. Little did she know that he was quite handy with a ladder, but he'd save that quest for another day. "Not a problem. Jennie?" he asked, looking around. "Where are the lights?"

Jennie popped up from her place on Joshua's rug and rustled the plastic bag that she'd sneaked past Claire.

"Right here. We didn't bring anything else in case you had ornaments, but if you don't have those, we'll give you some of ours. We always have plenty, right, Dad?"

"We have more than enough to go around." He turned to Claire. "I'll check these if you could bring water to keep the trunk from drying out."

It seemed strange to take charge in Claire's home, but she obviously was too overcome or too surprised to think of the necessities. "Water. Of course I'll bring water," she said before she hurried away.

Alex tightened the screws holding the tree upright in its stand, watching Joshua as he did so. The youngster had knelt on his toy rug, his little feet crossed behind him, as he pondered the scene in undisguised curiosity. Later, after Alex had plugged the cord in the electrical socket and the multicolored lights began to twinkle, delight covered Joshua's face.

If Alex had harbored any doubts about his decision, Josh's excitement made them magically disappear.

He wanted Claire to see his expression for herself, and a minute later fate granted his wish. Claire stopped in the doorway and stared at her son. The lines on her face softened until a smile tugged at her mouth.

He'd done the right thing.

She came forward, carrying a small pitcher. As soon as Joshua noticed her, he pointed to the corner. "Twee."

"A Christmas tree," Jennie corrected. "And we're going to make it be-ooo-tiful."

"Boo-ful," Joshua echoed.

While Alex began installing the lights, Claire knelt down, pushed a few branches out of the way and carefully added the water to the base.

A few minutes later, his job was done and he stepped back to view his handiwork. The lights flashed on and off against the dark green boughs. "If you want more—"

"No, it looks great the way it is. I can tell you've done this before," Claire teased.

"Once or twice," he admitted.

Jennie clapped her hands. "Isn't it pretty?"

Not to be outdone, Joshua clapped, too.

"I'd say we're finished here," Alex said. "Next stop, our house." He looked at Claire and raised one eyebrow. "You're still coming, aren't you?"

He held his breath, hoping that she wouldn't change her mind.

She nodded slowly. "Yes. I'm looking forward to it."

"So am I," he said, fervently. "So am I."

Alex's house was a sprawling brick home that was much larger and clearly more expensive than hers. Oak furnishings matched the oak woodwork, and deep, masculine colors of navy, burgundy and forest green created a restful atmosphere.

At the moment, the state of his living room was in the exact condition Claire had pictured. Decorations were draped over the sides of several large cartons and tissue paper was strewn across the floor. At first Joshua was content sitting on her lap as he watched Jennie and Alex add strings of gold beads and garlands to the tree that towered above him. Then Jennie gave him a candy cane to hang, and after that he wasn't content with his former spectator status.

"Me," he demanded, holding out his hand for something else to suspend from the tree. Naturally, he placed his ornaments in a bunch on the bottom branch, but when he wasn't looking, Jennie swiftly spread them around. If Joshua wondered where his pretty baubles went, he didn't appear to care.

Every now and then, he would help himself to the bite-sized cheese crackers that Alex had provided but, after eating a few, he was always ready to resume his decorating duties.

Claire sipped mulled cider and simply enjoyed watching the others work. On more than one occasion, she blinked back a tear as Alex hoisted Joshua in the air so he could place an ornament near the top.

Joshua screamed with delight.

He might not remember this particular day in the years ahead, but Claire would always carry this sight with her.

Maybe Ray wasn't the man who'd share these times with his son, but she couldn't have asked for a better man than Alex to take his place.

Soon, Alex declared the boxes empty. "That's it. We're done."

Joshua peered over the edge of the carton to see for himself. "Done?"

"All done," Alex echoed.

"I'm going to take Joshua to my room," Jennie announced as she held out her hand to him. "I want to read some of my books to him."

"Watch the steps," Alex admonished.

"I will. Come, Joshie."

Claire helped restore Alex's living room, then settled against the sofa cushions with her refilled mug. "Thanks for the afternoon. Joshua really enjoyed it."

"I'm glad. And did Joshua's mother enjoy herself, too?"

More than she probably should have, although Nora and Claire's family would disagree. "Yes," she said simply.

He grinned. "Good, because the clinic is next."

Although she'd slept reasonably well last night at the hospital, she knew she'd need a nap, too, if Alex was determined to tackle that project as well.

"Shouldn't we save some of the fun for tomorrow?" she asked.

He shook his head. "Nope. We're on a roll. Didn't your

mother tell you not to put off until tomorrow what you can do today?''

"Yes, but Christmas decorating didn't fall in that category."

He shrugged. "Maybe not, but there's a law at work at our house. The number of medical emergencies I have is directly proportional to the number of jobs waiting at home. So I do what I can *when* I can."

"Is that why a man who's been divorced for seven years spends his Saturday evenings alone? So he can catch up on his chores?"

"I'm not alone," he protested mildly. "I have you, and Joshua, and Jennie."

"Tonight you do, but what about other Saturdays? You've surely kicked up your heels. All work and no play makes Alex a dull boy."

"I haven't been a total hermit," he protested. "I've gone out on a number of occasions. Jennie never seemed to strike a chord with the women I dated, so they simply faded away. They were great ladies, but I wasn't interested enough in them to force the issue."

"Jennie's very protective of you. She told me some time ago that she doesn't need a mother."

"So she says. I've bent over backward to compensate for both her physical problems and for Donna walking out on her. I may have done us both a disservice."

"I wouldn't worry. She seems like a healthy, wholesome little girl to me. I hope I raise Joshua as well. By the way, I'm really amazed at how patient Jennie is with him."

"Jennie likes preschool children. Probably because they'll do what she tells them." He grinned.

Joshua's sudden howl brought Claire to the edge of her seat. Before she could stand, Joshua tottered in, tugging on his ear lobe.

Jennie followed, clearly worried. "He didn't hurt his

ear, honest. We were playing and all of a sudden he looked around and started crying.''

Joshua ran into Claire's outstretched arms and she wiped away the two trails of tears on his rosy cheeks. "He's OK, Jennie," she told her. "When he's tired, he pulls on his ear. He'll be fine after he sleeps for a few hours. Alex, I'm sorry, but decorating the clinic will have to wait."

Without asking, Alex fetched their coats and helped her with hers. His gentlemanly courtesy was unexpected but appreciated as he stood close enough behind her for his breath to caress her neck. She sensed that, if not for their audience, he might have pulled her against him as he had earlier.

She wouldn't have objected in the least.

Slowly, hesitantly, she moved away, certain that she'd seen the same reluctance in his dark eyes.

"Drive carefully," he said as he handed over Joshua's coat and hat.

"We're only going a few blocks," she reminded him. It had been a long time since someone, other than Nora or her brother, had expressed concern over her well-being. "And it's still daylight."

"You never know," he said.

Claire said her goodbyes, Joshua waved his, and they soon headed for home.

Alex didn't close the door until Claire had pulled out of his driveway. "That was fun," he said to Jennie.

"It was," she agreed. "It would be nice to have a little brother like Joshua."

Alex was surprised to hear Jennie broach the subject. She'd never asked for a sibling before. "Do you think so?"

"Yeah. It's fun, teaching him things."

He decided to test the waters. "You can't have a brother or a sister without having a mother."

"But I don't want a mother."

"Why not?"

"We have Mrs Rowe. And I'm eight. I don't need a mom like Joshua does."

He shrugged as if the subject was insignificant when to him it was anything but. Until Claire had arrived, he hadn't realized how his days had passed by in a haze of sameness. Now he felt alive, *awakened,* and he didn't want to regress.

"Someday you may change your mind," he said, mentally crossing his fingers that she would. Perhaps the time spent with Claire would convince her.

As for himself, after a dry spell of five long years since his last semi-serious date, he didn't want to be alone. He'd do whatever it took for Claire to end up in his Christmas stocking.

CHAPTER SEVEN

"I JUST walked past the waiting room and once I did, I simply had to talk to you," Nora said early on Monday morning. "Our tree looks fantastic!"

Claire looked up from her task of restocking drawers with their pap smear supplies to smile at her friend. "Thanks. I think so, too."

"That ribbon with the snowflakes is an absolute inspiration. And who would have thought to drape blue and silver curling ribbon over the branches?" Nora shook her head. "If we don't win a prize of some sort, I'll be surprised. This is so *unusual.*"

"Do you think so?"

"Without a doubt. Your plan was an absolute stroke of genius."

"What plan?"

"Didn't you know that each department decorates their trees on Wednesday and then, before everyone leaves, they scope out the others? Of course, they're not allowed to look until their own is finished because once they do, they can't work on theirs again."

"I didn't know that." What a stroke of luck that she hadn't walked through the clinic last Wednesday evening but, then, she'd been too stressed to care what everyone else had done.

"Anyway, I'm sure if the rest of the staff saw ours, they would have gotten overconfident. I don't mind telling you, it looked a little plain when I left, but now? Our tree could be on the cover of a magazine."

"Don't be ridiculous. We only added the bows and curling ribbon."

"And the silver berries. It might not have been much, but it was definitely enough to make it *dazzling*." Nora hugged her. "I knew you hadn't completely lost your Christmas spirit. It was just buried. You did a fabulous job."

Claire grinned. "Only because I had help from Alex and Jennie."

"Speaking of those two, what's this I hear about them delivering an evergreen to your house? My neighbor works at the lot where they bought it and he told me what Alex had done."

Claire flipped through the morning lab reports that had just come over the fax machine. "They brought it for Joshua."

"Isn't that sweet?"

"We only strung lights," she warned, "so don't imagine some awesome creation. My old decorations are still in storage."

"What are you waiting for?"

Courage, flashed into Claire's mind. Rather than say so, she said, "A moment to call my own." She outlined the weekend's events, from visiting Alex's house to sewing Jennie's costume on Sunday and finishing the tree.

"So you're getting along with his daughter, are you?"

"Why wouldn't I?"

"No reason, other than that's the best news I've heard in a month. She doesn't usually take a shine to the women he's dated."

"We're not dating, so it doesn't matter." Deep down, though, it did.

"That might be what you think, but we'll save that conversation for another day. Right now, I want to know what you're going to wear to the clinic party."

"I haven't thought about it because I intend to play hookey."

Nora stared at her in horror. "You can't."

"Why not? Henry will understand." At least, she hoped he would.

"You've come so far. You can't quit now."

"Watch me."

"Now, Claire—"

"Now, Claire nothing," Claire said. "Be satisfied with the progress I've made. Between decorating trees and owning a live one myself, I'm showing more Christmas spirit than I'd intended when the season started."

Nora opened her mouth to argue, then clamped her lips together. "OK. If that's how you feel. Just remember, though, you'll miss the perfect opportunity to wear your fanciest dress and watch Alex's eyes pop out of his head."

If she wore her fanciest gown, then Alex would wear his best suit. The prospect of seeing him decked out was the one thing that could change her mind about going. Although she wasn't actively hunting for a man to take Ray's place, Alex was the only potential candidate who'd hammered home the fact that she was still young and possessed an adequate amount of female hormones.

If only her femininity had waited to awaken until after the holidays.

"Sorry, but Christmas parties are out. I can't walk into a room filled with couples. I just can't."

"So go with Alex instead of going alone."

Alex. It had been wonderful being in his arms for those few minutes. She'd felt warm and safe and guilt-free and now that she thought about it, she'd actually felt whole.

Whole. It had been so long since she'd experienced that, but now that she had, it only emphasized her loss.

Darn the holidays with their associated hugging and kissing and good cheer!

She dumped several more kits and disposable speculums into the deep middle drawer to avoid Nora's gaze. "He hasn't asked me."

"That's easily remedied. Ask him instead."

"I can't."

"Why not?"

"I just can't, so let's leave it at that."

"Then I'll—"

"Don't you dare take matters in your own hands, Nora Laslow. If you do, I'll never speak to you again."

Nora held up her hands. "OK. I heard you. Loud and clear."

"Good." Claire closed the drawer with a sharp snap.

Nora fell silent for a few seconds, but when she spoke again, she sounded puzzled. "Don't you *want* to go with him?"

Claire hesitated. "That's not the point."

"Aha! I knew it! You *do*."

Once again, Claire didn't answer directly. She would dearly love to go out with Alex, but she was thinking along the lines of a quiet dinner for two, not a boisterous affair with several hundred people.

"*If*—" she emphasized the word "—I decide to attend, I'll go by myself because I'll only stay long enough to put in my duty appearance. I won't have someone taking me as his date and then spoiling his fun by cutting the evening short."

Nora didn't need to know that she'd prefer being at home to seeing another woman on Alex's arm.

You're hiding.

Claire ignored her little voice that sounded remarkably like Alex.

"You're forgetting one key detail," Nora said.

"What?"

"If you come with Alex, you wouldn't *want* to just pop in and out. You'd *want* to stay, sip champagne, eat choc-olate-covered strawberries and dance until midnight."

"Champagne and strawberries?"

"None other."

Claire smiled. "Remember when we bought our first bottle to celebrate passing our state nursing boards?"

"As if I'd ever forget. You complained the entire time about how the bubbles tickled your nose, but it didn't stop you from drinking your half."

"Yeah, and I can't believe we measured it out in a specimen cup to make sure we each drank the same amount."

"It was an experiment," Nora said importantly. "If you'll recall, we were trying to determine the effects of alcohol on different body types."

"What did we decide?"

Nora waved her hand. "Who cares? We had fun. And you will, too, when you come to the clinic party."

"Sorry, pal, but it will take more than champagne to get me there," Claire said.

Offering champagne was probably the worst thing Nora could have used as temptation. She and Ray had celebrated the milestones of their marriage with it—his first decent-paying job, their mortgage, the night she'd told him she was pregnant. Of course, she'd only taken a few swallows at the time, but a toast had been part of their ritual—a ritual that had ended years too soon.

She'd bought a bottle of bubbly before she'd gone into labor and on her first night home, after Joshua had fallen asleep in his crib, she'd sat on the sofa in front of the fireplace—Ray's favorite spot—managed to pop the cork and fill two glasses before she sipped a toast to her missing husband and the precious gift he'd given her. Then she'd cried the rest of the night.

The next morning, she'd poured out the contents of his full glass along with the remainder of the bottle and concentrated on caring for her son. She'd done well these past three years, but Christmas still pressed a sore spot.

In any event, she doubted if she'd ever be able to look at champagne in the same way again.

"If the drinks won't entice you, maybe the food will.

It's going to be utterly fantastic.'' Nora patted her tummy.
"I should know because I signed up for the catering committee, which was fun since I didn't have to worry about
paying the bill.'' She grinned. "I made sure we would
serve something that would tempt you into coming. The
hors d'oeuvres are spectacular and if you're not interested
in those, the dessert bar will feature six different kinds of
cheesecake, including your favorite, chocolate caramel.''

"The menu sounds fabulous, but my mind is made up.''

"If you don't want a date and you don't want to go by
yourself, why don't you come with Carter and me? I've
already arranged for a sitter, so you can leave Joshua with
my brood. One more won't make a difference to her. When
you're ready to call it a night, you can slip away.''

So much for her plan to use the can't-find-a-babysitter
excuse. "Thanks for the suggestion and the offer, but I
don't want to go. What would I do?''

Nora rolled her eyes. "Have fun?'' She raised her
hands. "I know, I know. You can't. What would an hour
hurt, though? If you promise to stay sixty minutes, I'll be
happy.''

"You're forgetting Henry's job list,'' Claire reminded
her.

"Volunteer to guard the eggnog,'' Nora advised. "I'll
take the other half of your shift and no one will be the
wiser.''

"And you'll be satisfied if I agree to one hour?''

"One hour *minimum* and I'll stop hounding you. For the
record, I'm counting from the moment you walk in to the
second you leave. Travel time is excluded.''

Claire grinned. "You drive a hard bargain, pal.''

"Yup, but I'm betting you'll want to stay longer.''

"You're on. What'll it be?''

"An afternoon of babysitting,'' Nora said promptly.

"You're going to lose.''

Nora gave her sly wink. "Maybe. Maybe not. This *is* the season for miracles."

Claire agreed in theory but, as far as she was concerned, there were far too many people who needed one more than she did. People like her next patient, Victor Kohls.

"My bowels just aren't working right," the seventy-two-year-old, frail-looking Victor said. "Haven't been for some time."

"How long?"

"Couple of months. It started with some diarrhea, but now…" he rubbed his abdomen "…it's the opposite."

"What kind of food do you eat? Lots of fiber? Fresh fruit and vegetables?"

"Apples, oranges—my wife even started giving me broccoli—cooked oatmeal and shredded wheat cereal. Lots of shredded wheat." He shook his head. "Nothing."

"What about over-the-counter fiber supplements?"

"The pharmacist suggested a powder to dump in my juice." He mentioned the brand name, which she noted. "But the only difference is I feel like I'm stuffed to my gills. Lost my appetite on account of it."

"When did you start adding a supplement?"

"Two weeks ago. Surely that high-powered, fancy fiber would have kicked in by now."

"You'd think so," she agreed.

"The trouble is, I'm losing weight that I can't afford to lose. Of course, it could be on account of not eating. Just don't want to."

"Have you been running a temperature?"

He screwed his aged face in thought. "No, but I have the chills from time to time. Just can't seem to get warm. Don't thyroid problems cause that?"

"They could," she admitted.

"What do you think is wrong?"

In Claire's opinion, it sounded like he had an obstructed bowel, but without further tests, it was anyone's guess what might be the cause. Everything from adhesions to a hernia, Crohn's disease to a case of fecal impaction came to mind. For his sake, she hoped it would be easily resolved.

"Well," she said slowly with a smile, "that's what you're paying the doctor to find out. Let's see what he says, OK?"

"OK."

If Alex had a ready diagnosis in mind, or even a suspicion of one, he kept it to himself, but Claire had worked with him long enough to recognize when he was concerned because his smile didn't reach his eyes.

"Do you have a history of colon problems in your family?" he asked after he'd read through Claire's notes.

Victor looked thoughtful. "Not that I can remember."

"Have you ever had a colonoscopy?"

"Isn't that when they run a tube up your, well…" He blushed a deep red as he glanced at Claire. "You know."

Alex grinned. "Yes."

Victor shook his head. "No, I haven't. Do I need that now?"

"It would be best," Alex told him. "A surgeon needs to look around in there."

"You can't do it?" he asked.

"It's a special procedure requiring special training. I'm going to refer you to Dr Jensen. Claire will set up the appointment."

A suspicious glint appeared in Victor's eyes. "Never heard of this Jensen fellow."

"It's a lady," Alex told him. "Susan Jensen. She joined Dr Teague's practice a few months ago."

"Why can't I see him instead? I'm not wild about having a lady look up my nether regions."

"You won't have to wait as long to see her as you will for an appointment with Dr Teague," Alex replied. "The sooner we find out what the problem is, the sooner we can correct it, and the sooner you can eat like your old self.''

Victor hesitated. ''I s'pose. And you say she's good?''

''Dr Teague wouldn't have taken her on as a partner if she wasn't.''

''If you say it's OK, Doctor, I'll do it.''

Alex scribbled something on a pad before he ripped off the page and handed it to Claire. ''Before you leave, my nurse will set up a time for you to see Dr Jensen,'' he informed Victor.

Claire took the slip of paper and saw written there, ''ASAP. R/o CA.'' All of which was shorthand for hurry up, and rule out carcinoma.

''Will this lady doctor tell you what she finds?''

''Oh, yes.''

''What do I do in the meantime?''

''Eat what you feel you can tolerate. I'd stay away from high-fiber foods, though.''

''You don't have to tell me twice,'' Victor said fervently.

''OK. Wait here until Claire tells you about your appointment with Dr Jensen.''

Claire made her phone call and, after explaining the situation, was given a time slot. She returned to Victor's room, smiling brightly.

''It's your lucky day,'' she informed him.

''I could use a fair bit of luck,'' Victor told her. ''I'm not Irish, but I'm ready to claim some of theirs.''

''They had a cancellation this afternoon. You can see Dr Jensen at one-thirty.''

''Are they going to do my colon thing then?''

''No,'' Claire told him. ''You'll need to prepare for the procedure, but Dr Jensen's office will explain everything. Today she wants to meet you, describe what will happen and talk about what she might find.''

"Like polyps? My neighbor had a couple of those removed last summer."

"Yes," she said.

"Will she do this in her office?"

"Usually she performs this procedure at the hospital. You'll only be there for a few hours, so you'll go to the day surgery floor. You'll receive medication to relax you, so be sure someone will be available to drive you home."

"I'll ask my son," he decided. "The wife doesn't drive any more."

"Dr Jensen's office nurse will give you more dos and don'ts. Just be sure you don't miss your appointment."

"At one-thirty. I'll be there."

Claire sent him on his way, then called for Rick Morris. A handsome man in his late thirties with a ruddy complexion, a muscular build and sturdy denim clothing that suggested a manual labor job, he slowly rose from his chair in the waiting room and advanced with what seemed a great deal of reluctance until Claire realized it was more of an unsteady gait. His wife walked beside him, chattering away as if she didn't have a care in the world, but Claire saw the worry lines on her forehead.

After helping him step carefully on the scale, Claire showed him to the closest exam room and listened to his story.

"My feet tingle all the time, like someone's sticking hundred of pins in them," Rick reported. "I have times when I'm dizzy and my vision blurs, but then it goes away."

"Have you noticed feeling weak?"

He flexed his left hand. "My hand doesn't seem to have the strength it used to."

"Now, Rick," his wife chided, "tell her how it goes numb."

"Once in a while," he admitted. "I just feel stiff. My

joints don't seem to move as easily as they once did. I'm thinking it might be arthritis.''

"It's a possibility," Claire said. "What about pain?"

"No pain as such, although when I get that pins-and-needles sensation, it isn't too pleasant."

Claire added a few more notes to her list of reported symptoms. "Anything else?"

His wife answered. "He seems more jittery. At times, he even seems depressed."

Rick glowered at her, as if she wasn't supposed to notice that particular sign. "You'd be depressed, too, if you didn't feel right."

"That's quite true," Claire said. "How long have you felt this way?"

"It's come and gone for a couple of months, so at first I thought it was just a weird virus and ignored it."

"He's had it long enough that we can't," his wife added. "The last two weeks have been the worst and I decided it was time we came to the doctor."

"We?" Rick raised an eyebrow at his wife. "*I'm* the one who'll be poked and prodded."

"If that's what it takes to figure out why you're like this, quit complaining," she said, exasperated.

Claire sympathized with Rick's wife. Men weren't easy creatures to be around when they were ill and obviously Rick hadn't felt well for some time. "Had you been sick with anything in particular before you noticed these symptoms?"

He shook his head. "Not that I can remember."

Claire finished her notes, then walked around the exam table to wrap the blood-pressure cuff around his arm. "I'll take a few readings," she said as she pumped air into the cuff, "and then send in the doctor."

His vital signs were within normal limits and she soon returned with Alex.

"Hello, Joyce," he greeted Rick's wife.

"Alex," she said, relief obvious in her tone. "It's good to see you. This is my husband, Rick."

Alex shook his hand. "How's Wendy? I haven't seen her for a while."

Claire followed their conversation and soon figured out that Rick was Joyce's second husband, and that Wendy and Jennie were classmates, but this year they'd suffered the misfortune of being assigned to different teachers. Although they chatted for only a few minutes, Claire could see Rick's growing irritation.

Alex apparently sensed the same thing, because he deftly turned the conversation to Rick. "You're having muscle weakness?"

At which point Rick began his recitation. Alex listened carefully before he asked more in-depth questions.

"Any trouble with bladder or bowel control?" he asked.

"Can't hold my water like I used to," Rick admitted. "If the urge hits, I'd better take care of business, or else."

"Does temperature make a difference?" Alex asked. "Hot or cold?"

"Not that I can tell."

"Do you drink alcohol?"

Joyce studied the tile floor while her husband answered. "Yeah."

"How much?"

Rick bristled. "What difference does it make?"

That particular subject was a sore one. Claire watched to see how Alex would handle his patient.

"A lot," Alex answered bluntly. "Alcoholism can cause a number of conditions or make certain ones worse. If you drink consistently, I need to know."

Rick fell silent. "Yeah, I drink. Some."

From the way Joyce had fixed her gaze on the floor, Claire suspected that "some" was probably an understatement.

"How much?" Alex asked.

"A six-pack on weeknights."

"What about weekends?"

Rick shrugged. "Two. Sometimes more. It depends."

Apparently satisfied by Rick's admission, Alex continued with his questions and examination.

"So what's wrong with me?" Rick asked when he'd finished.

"It could be a number of things," Alex said. "First I want blood tests to check for the obvious."

"What's the obvious?" Joyce asked.

"Anemia, infection, thyroid problems, diabetes," Alex replied. "We'll also see if we can rule out things like rheumatoid arthritis, lupus and other immune diseases."

"What if my tests don't show anything?"

"Then we'll keep looking. But I'll warn you, I'm going to order a lot of things right away, so don't panic if the lab folks take several large tubes of blood."

Rick nodded.

"I'd like you to go to the clinic lab next," Alex told him. "I'll fax my order to them, so they'll know what I want. I should have the results in a few days, so let's plan on seeing you toward the end of this week."

"I'll make sure he's here," Joyce said. "Thanks."

Alex smiled. "Tell Wendy not to be a stranger."

Claire followed him into their small medication room where she spent most of her time when she wasn't with patients. As soon as he'd finished writing in Rick's medical record, he handed it to her.

She scanned the list. CBC, comprehensive chemistry panel with CPK—she'd expected that test because it was a muscle enzyme test—panels for rheumatoid arthritis, lupus and thyroid function, vitamin B12 and folate. She looked up. "What do you think he has?"

"It's hard to say at this point. Ask me again after the lab sends the results." He grinned.

"Don't worry, I will." While Alex steadily ploughed

through his list of patients, he did so with half his mind on his most pressing problem.

Claire.

He wanted to ask her to accompany him to the clinic's party but, after overhearing her conversation with Nora, he knew her answer would be a polite but resounding "no". He and Jennie had used Josh to bring a traditional Christmas tree into her house, but he couldn't use those tactics for the party. He had to think of a way to storm her last wall of defense.

The question was, what approach would work? Henry had helped by requiring all employees to attend, but Claire's one-hour time limit would be exactly one hour, not a minute more or less, when Alex wanted that hour to stretch into five or six.

What to do?

Talking wouldn't help. Clearly Nora had been singing this tune for weeks. No doubt, Claire's family had, too. No, he needed someone else. Someone who'd been there, done that.

The answer came when he saw Claire usher their last patient for the morning, Edwina Butler, into an exam room. He gave them a few minutes alone, then decided to enter before Claire had a chance to get away.

"How are you, Edwina?" he asked the mother-to-be.

"Other than feeling tired and fat, I'm fine."

"Where's Joe?"

"I made him wait outside. His hovering is about to drive me over the edge." Eddie's gentle smile contradicted her exasperated tone.

"He's only concerned."

She sighed. "I know. I sometimes wonder if he wouldn't be quite so protective if I hadn't lost our last baby at Christmas-time."

Although Alex knew the exact details of Eddie's medical history and remembered her reaction when he'd first calculated the baby's due date, from the way Claire stiffened, she obviously had not known about it.

"I'm sorry to hear that," she murmured.

Alex took his time listening to the baby's foetal heart tones and hoped Eddie would keep talking. She did.

"It was bad enough losing the first one, but when it happened again, and during the holidays no less, it was even worse. Now I'm believing that our little bundle of joy this Christmas will make up for the previous ones."

"I'm sure that he or she will," Claire said. "I understand how hard it must have been."

"It was worse than hard," Eddie said cheerfully. "I couldn't stand to visit my family and see my sisters' little ones. Months later, I finally worked past that, but when it got closer to Christmas I dreaded the thought of it rolling around again."

"What did you do?" Alex asked, hoping she would explain, not only for Claire's sake but for the sake of his other patients who shared this sad experience.

"Nothing at first," Eddie said ruefully. "After I-don't-know-how-many therapy sessions with my minister, he finally said something that soaked in."

"What?" he encouraged.

"I had to give myself permission to enjoy Christmas. Hating it, being miserable, and doing everything I could think of to avoid it, wouldn't bring my baby back. He also said that I, as the wife and mother, set the tone for the household. What child, especially one in heaven, wants his or her mom to be miserable, much less to be miserable at Christmas?"

"He sounds like an insightful man," Alex said, watching Claire out of the corner of his eye.

"He is," Eddie agreed. "Once I decided that he was right, and I wasn't being fair to Joe or myself, I sat down one afternoon and followed his advice."

"And it worked?"

"Yeah. I still had bad moments, but they didn't last long. I didn't recover overnight, but gradually I coped."

"I'm glad."

"What amazes me is what happened a few months after I made that choice." Her tummy moved as her child obviously stretched, and she rubbed the spot. "A miracle came our way."

Alex straightened. "Well, your little miracle seems to be doing fine. I'll see you next week, if not before."

"She might come early?" Eddie's face shone with excitement.

"He or she might," he said as he helped her to a sitting position.

"My word! Wait until I tell Joe." With that, she scooted off the table and hurried from the room.

Claire hadn't moved. "How could you?" she demanded.

"How could I what?" he asked, although he knew what she meant.

She waved her arms wildly. "Get Eddie to talk about her baby and Christmas. Did you plan this ahead of time?"

"You saw her before I did," he said calmly. "If I'd known how to raise the subject, I would have, but she started talking on her own. Remember? I'll admit I kept the conversation going, but I didn't write the dialog ahead of time."

Claire's anger faded before his eyes. "Why?" Her voice sounded as if tears clogged her throat. "Why should you care if I celebrate Christmas or not?"

Alex moved closer and, grabbing her hand, pulled her into a loose embrace. "Because I want you in my life," he said simply. "I want you to go with me to the clinic party and be there from start to finish."

"Oh, Alex." She shook her head. "I don't think I can."

"I happen to disagree." He hesitated. "I overheard what

you told Nora, and I'm selfish enough to want to convince you by any means available. If I have to use Eddie, I will.

"You know what I want and you heard Eddie's advice. Think about both, weigh what was said and when you've come to a decision, let me know." He cupped her chin. "I'll be waiting."

CHAPTER EIGHT

HE'LL be waiting until hell freezes over, Claire silently fumed as she stormed out and sought sanctuary in an empty exam room. Maybe Alex hadn't orchestrated the scene she'd landed in, but the fact that he would have if he could have irritated her all the more.

He only wants to take you to the party, her little voice chided.

And I don't want to go, she mentally answered. I want to be left alone, to spend the holiday as I choose.

To feel miserable? It won't bring Ray back.

Those words seemed to echo in her head before she acknowledged the answer.

No, it wouldn't change the fact that Ray was gone, but was the answer to her own dilemma as simple as Eddie had made it sound? To simply grant herself permission to enjoy everything the season offered? To enjoy all twelve months, instead of only eleven?

You came here to start over, remember?

She remembered, but it had become habit to associate Christmas with sadness. The thought had barely had time to soak in before she realized one key word.

Habit.

It wasn't habit, she insisted to herself. Ray's death had robbed her of her joy of the season, but even as she thought of the way she'd once eagerly anticipated the hustle and bustle of Christmas, she could hear Ray's favorite expression.

You're not making lemonade with your lemons, Claire.

He'd been a man who'd rolled with the punches and believed life was for living.

He'd certainly lived it to the fullest, she thought as she recalled one evening in particular. She'd been busy preparing dinner so they could go to the early show that evening, but in the middle of trying to do three things at once, Ray had come in, taken the spoon out of her hand, shut off the stove top and playfully tugged her onto their patio with its westerly view.

"You can't miss this sunset," he'd said.

"But our dinner," she'd wailed. "It'll be ruined, and we'll be late."

"Sometimes food for the soul is better than food for the body," he'd said before he'd pointed out the spectacular hues in the sky. "As for being late, I don't think any movie can top this."

He'd been right. In the end, they'd stayed outside long past the time when their meal could be salvaged. They'd even missed both showings that night, but she'd never regretted their change of plans.

Life *was* too short to waste a single moment of it, Claire decided. No matter how hard she'd tried to ignore Christmas, it couldn't be ignored. If following Eddie's advice helped her jump over this final hurdle, she would.

She closed her eyes and said the necessary words aloud.

Peace immediately flooded over her. The tension she felt from the day when stores began stocking Christmas items disappeared and she hugged her new-found contentment to herself.

She wanted to tell Alex of her revelation, but chose to wait. She had one more Ghost of Christmas Past to lay to rest.

Alex tried to read the evening paper, but the words could have been Egyptian hieroglyphics for all the sense he made of the headlines. He'd intended to gently nudge Claire forward, much like he and Jennie had done with the tree, but he was afraid he'd shoved instead, putting more pressure on her than she could tolerate.

After the incident with Edwina Butler, Claire had kept to herself as she'd carried out her duties, much like when she'd first come to work at the clinic. He was sorry to see her revert to her all-professional demeanor, but he hoped it meant she was simply weighing everything she'd heard from him and from Eddie, not thinking of a way to tell him to find another Christmas-party date.

She'd avoided his gaze all afternoon, although after he'd finished seeing the fifteen-year-old with athlete's foot, he'd noticed something in her eyes that suggested she'd come to a crossroads. Curiosity was killing him now, just as it had at the time, but he couldn't do anything about it. He'd told Claire to let him know of her decision and, as difficult as it was to be patient, he had to wait. If Lady Luck was on his side, he'd eventually hear good news.

"Daddy," Jennie said, "the buzzer buzzed. Our dinner's ready."

He folded the newsprint into a neat rectangle. "It smells good. Did you help Mrs Rowe cook?"

"No. I had to do my homework early 'cause we're going over to Claire's. She still has to hem my costume, remember?"

As if he could forget. He usually kept Joshua occupied with toys or a story so Claire and Jennie could work uninterrupted but, all things considered, it might not be a good idea for him to appear on her doorstep tonight. Lying low, giving her space might do more for his cause than not, but would changing their routine hinder or help matters?

"I remember," he told her.

"Wendy said at recess that her stepfather is sick. Is he going to die?" Jennie asked.

Alex spooned a serving of beef and noodle casserole onto Jennie's plate. "I'm not expecting him to. Why?"

"Just wondering. Wendy doesn't like him much. She says he's mean to her and her mom, especially when he's been drinking."

He wasn't surprised. "Some people aren't very nice when they don't feel well."

"I don't think he's nice when he feels good," Jennie said. "He's always yelling. He even yells when I'm there."

This subject was like quicksand and, rather than find himself sucked into its depths, Alex gave it a wide berth. "Wendy's mother wouldn't have married him if he didn't have good qualities."

"Wendy says he was nicer before they got married than he is now."

"Unfortunately, that happens. Sometimes you can't see the other person's true colors until after the honeymoon is over." He could certainly speak from experience. He hadn't realized his ex-wife had been so shallow until their beautiful but flawed Jennie had arrived. He was glad that Donna had left their lives as totally as she had. He'd done everything he could to foster a positive self-image in his daughter and it wasn't beyond the realm of possibility that Donna would have undermined his efforts if she'd stayed.

He glanced at the kitchen clock. "We'd better hurry if we're going to be at Claire's by seven."

Twenty minutes later, after piling the dishes in the sink to soak, they were on their way. Those few blocks seemed like miles as one thought ran through his head.

Please, let her say yes.

Claire sat on the living-room floor, surrounded by the decorations she'd hauled in from the web-infested corner of the garage. This time, as she opened each package, the sight of their contents evoked more sweet than bitter memories, but the final test would be the long box at the bottom.

Joshua toddled back and forth from Claire to the tree, affixing the ornaments she handed him to the branches in haphazard order. When he returned for his next ball and she didn't have it ready, he grunted and stomped one foot.

"Sorry," she said. "I'll hurry."

After several more trips and apparently deciding that he didn't need her help, he simply pulled a ball from the box and set it on the branch. When it fell off and rolled under the tree, he bellowed his displeasure.

"Hang on," she told him as she retrieved the shiny red ornament.

Finally, the branches were loaded to Claire's satisfaction and only the very top remained unadorned. Sitting on the sofa, she carefully opened the last box and removed the angel.

Joshua climbed beside her. Standing on the seat cushion, with one hand on her shoulder for balance, he touched the angel's hair. "Mama."

She hugged him. "The angel looks like Mama, doesn't she? Should we put her on top of the tree?"

"Top," he demanded.

Claire placed the angel in Joshua's hands, then carried him to the tree where he placed it, with her help, in the highest place of honor.

He clapped his hands and chortled. "Pwetty angel."

"Pretty tree."

He leaned over and kissed her sloppily. "Pwetty Mama."

She laughed and nuzzled his neck. "Thank you, my handsome little man."

The doorbell chimed and she glanced at the clock. "That must be Jennie."

"'Ennie play." Joshua squirmed and tried to dive to the floor.

"I have to fix her costume first," she told him.

"'Les play," he said in an obvious reference to Alex.

"I'm sure he will."

It suddenly occurred to Claire that he might not stay like he usually did, that he might feel too uncomfortable in light of her attitude this afternoon. Determined to stop him from leaving if that was his intent, she hurried to the door and flung it open.

As she saw Alex standing next to Jennie, she'd never felt more relieved. "You're right on time." She smiled as she welcomed them inside and took their coats.

Alex motioned to the boxes resting in the center of her living room. "Looks like you're in the middle of something. If you want us to come back later…"

"No," she said as she hung Jennie's coat in the closet. "Joshua and I just finished."

"Dad!" Jennie exclaimed from the living room. "You have to come and see."

Claire followed Alex and watched him study the tree before his attention seemed to linger on the angel. "You did a beautiful job." He turned to her. "I thought you weren't going to decorate it."

Suddenly feeling nervous, she folded her arms across her chest. "I changed my mind."

"Obviously."

"Ray and I bought the angel a few weeks before he died. It was time to let Joshua appreciate it."

"He will."

"It looks better on a taller pine, but there's always next year," she said, wishing she could read Alex's thoughts.

"Maybe you can get one as big as ours," Jennie said.

"We might. We'll need help to get it through the door, though." Claire met Alex's gaze and wondered if he'd heard the hopeful invitation in her voice.

"We'll help, won't we, Dad?"

Alex's regard didn't waver. "I can't wait."

Joshua tugged on Jennie's hand. "Dwink," he said. "Firsty."

She glanced at Claire. "Is it OK if I pour him a drink?" At her nod, Jennie led Joshua into the kitchen.

"My daughter's making herself at home," Alex said. "I hope you don't mind."

"Not at all." She wanted him to say something else, but he didn't. He wasn't going to make this easy, she thought, but, then, he'd made it clear that the next move would be hers.

"I'm sure you're wondering what brought this on," she said, motioning to the tree.

"I'll admit to a certain curiosity." Alex sounded wary, as if he was afraid he might jump to the wrong conclusion.

"You see," she began slowly, "I heard some good advice today and I decided to take it." She squared her shoulders and hoped he would read the reassurance in her eyes. "I also decided something else."

"Like what?" He still sounded cautious.

She inhaled a deep breath. "I'd be honored to go to the clinic party with you next weekend."

A wide grin spread across his face. "I'd crossed my fingers all day, praying to hear you say that. You won't regret it," he promised.

"No," she answered softly. "I don't think I will."

"Are you sure your mother doesn't mind watching Joshua, too?" Claire asked Alex as he parked in front of his house on the night of the clinic's annual holiday event. "I hate to impose."

"She was delighted," he told her. "It's been so long since there's been a baby in the family that she could hardly wait to get her hands on one."

"I should have dropped him off at Nora's instead," she insisted. Leaving Joshua with Alex's mother might plant a few ideas in people's heads, and if his mother was like hers, he'd endure sly winks and Cheshire-cat smiles in the weeks and months to come.

"We've worked this out," he said patiently. "Every-one's happy about the arrangement. Jennie is thrilled; my mother is looking forward to a good cuddle; and knowing her the way I do, Jennie and Josh will have a wonderful time and fall asleep exhausted. Trust me."

"All right."

"Good. Now I'll get Josh and you grab his bag."

He'd cleared his sidewalk so the surface wasn't slippery from their early morning dusting of snow, otherwise Claire would have had trouble navigating the distance in her dressiest footwear. She was used to wearing comfortable shoes with an arch support, not these black pumps with their low but narrow heels.

Inside Alex's home, she dug Joshua out of his blanket cocoon. As soon as he saw Jennie, a smile spread from ear to ear and he followed her like a child after the Pied Piper.

"You must be Claire," Eleanor Ridgeway said as she came from the living room to greet her.

Claire smiled at the woman who was tall, stately, and every bit as distinguished as her handsome son. "I'm pleased to meet you, Mrs Ridgeway."

"Please, call me Eleanor. Don't worry about young Joshua a bit. We're going to get along famously. I taught preschool for years so I've learned a few tricks of the trade."

"Joshua doesn't take long to warm to people," Claire said. "He's used to seeing new faces at his day care."

"Excellent! Now, you two run along and have a won-derful time. If I need you, I have Alex's cell phone and pager numbers. Memorized, in fact."

"I packed Joshua's snuggle bunny," Claire said. "He won't go to sleep without it."

"I'll be sure he has it."

She glanced at Alex. "I guess that's everything." Oddly enough, in spite of getting caught up in the party fever affecting everyone at the clinic, she was still nervous about the upcoming evening. Attending this function with the most handsome bachelor in their organization was a heady experience. Even her punch-and-eggnog assignment didn't dampen her spirits because Alex had volunteered to be her partner.

"Then we're off," he said cheerfully.

It was the medical clinic's Christmas tradition to reserve the entire Pleasant Valley Country Club for their holiday bash, and as Alex drove onto the winding road that led to the front door, it was obvious someone had transformed the building into a magical place.

Garlands and white twinkly lights were wound around the pillars standing sentinel at the front door. Young men dressed in black coats and red bow-ties stood at the ready to whisk the cars away for the guests.

"I can't believe Henry agreed to foot the bill for valet parking," Claire said as their turn came.

"He's a firm believer in not drinking and driving," Alex said. "The staff is under strict orders not to hand over the keys to anyone who might be intoxicated. He insists the expense is worth every penny, and I agree. Can you imagine the public relations nightmare if someone from the clinic was involved in an alcohol-related accident?"

She shuddered. "I wouldn't want to walk in that person's shoes."

Inside the club, every surface was dripping with holly, pine boughs and garlands, twinkly lights and elegant red, gold and green satin bows. As he guided her to the room where they could check in their coats, she was extremely conscious of his arm hovering at her back.

What really sent her heart soaring was the look of appreciation in Alex's eyes once she'd removed her coat. It was the same look she'd seen when he'd arrived at her house and it held enough heat to compensate for what her gown didn't cover.

Nora had insisted on shopping for a special dress and they'd found a sleeveless, low-cut white beaded top that was the perfect match for an ankle-length slim, black shimmery skirt. According to the sales clerk, the slit down one side revealed enough thigh to dazzle her date.

From Alex's expression, the woman had been right.

He was no slouch in the dressing department either. His black suit jacket stretched across broad shoulders and his pleated trousers clung to powerful legs. To Claire, he simply outshone every other male in the room and the realization made it nearly impossible for her to think and breathe at the same time.

Inside the ballroom, the decorating committee had outdone themselves. The room had been transformed into a winter wonderland scene, complete with sheer blue and silver ribbon streamers, blue and silver balloons, blue candles surrounded by fake snow on every table, and what had to be miles and miles of twinkly lights.

A swan ice sculpture stood in the center of a buffet table loaded with artfully arranged finger food. A string quartet played softly in the background, although later in the evening a jazz band was to replace them.

In spite of her three-year hiatus, company Christmas parties hadn't changed. Conversation hummed, glassware clinked, laughter occasionally broke out, and women wore glittery gowns that hadn't left their closets since the previous December.

Claire leaned closer to Alex. "Are the parties always this impressive?"

"I've only been to one other, but it was definitely on the same grand scale. Shall we mingle before we take over our serving duties, or eat first?"

"Eat," she said promptly.

"A woman after my own heart," he said as he guided her to the buffet.

After Claire had filled her plate with everything from

jumbo shrimp to bite-sized cheesecakes, she stopped by the beverage table where Nora and their receptionist, Roberta, were filling glass cups with non-alcoholic punch or eggnog.

"How's business?" Claire asked Nora.

"Steady," she answered. "Can I give you a sample or are you going for the hard stuff?"

"Punch, please," Claire said.

"What about you?" Nora addressed Alex.

"The same."

Nora handed them each a cup, the handles facing them. "Part of our group latched onto a table near the north bar. There's plenty of room for you two."

"Great," Alex exclaimed.

"We'll expect you back in thirty minutes," Nora said. "So eat fast."

"We will," Claire promised.

Nora leaned closer. "Keep an eye on Eric."

Alex glanced over at their reserved spot and frowned. His height gave him an advantage over Claire because she couldn't see over the crowd, but whatever fell in Alex's line of vision clearly didn't please him. "Arrived early, did he?"

"Half an hour ago, but he's drinking champagne like it's water."

"Thanks for the warning," he answered.

"What's the matter with Dr Halverson?" Claire asked as they ambled through the crowd to reach the rest of the family practice group.

"The woman he's been living with issued an ultimatum yesterday."

"What sort of ultimatum?"

"Either he puts a ring on her finger or she's history."

"Ah. He's obviously alone, so I presume he's celebrating his new-found freedom?"

"It's more a case of drowning his sorrows," he corrected.

"Why? It's his decision, so he has no one to blame but himself."

"That's the problem. He's been married before and swore he never would be again. I think he really loves this gal, but he's afraid to commit." He greeted his partners and introduced Claire to Dennis's wife, Sharon, and Tanya, Mike's spouse. No one seemed surprised to see that Alex had brought Claire, which helped her to feel less like she was on display.

"Has anyone seen Henry?" he asked after they were seated.

Eric motioned to the stage with his champagne flute. "He was testing the microphone a few minutes ago."

"Who'll announce the winner of the decorating contest?" Tanya asked.

"Henry, his cronies and Dianne usually do," Eric said before he gestured to the waiter for a refill.

Dianne was the business director of the Pleasant Valley Clinic and rumor claimed that nothing happened, good or bad, big or little, without her knowledge.

"Hey, Eric," Mike said, "how many of those have you had?"

"Not enough." He accepted another glass. "But don't worry. When I hit my limit, I'll stop."

"How many is your limit?" Alex asked.

"I don't know, but when I decide, I'll let you know."

Claire heard the pain in his voice and wished she knew what to say. Everyone else obviously felt the same, because Eric's three partners exchanged uneasy glances.

"Hey, now," Eric protested. "Don't look so down in the dumps. It's a party. We're supposed to have fun. So let's toast." He raised his glass. "Let the good times roll." He drained the contents, then slammed the glass on the table.

His cheerful mood suddenly became solemn. "Oh, hell," he murmured. "Are we having fun yet?"

"You aren't," Alex said. "You need something to eat."

"Later." Eric glanced around the table. "First, I have a question to ask. You wives, go powder your noses."

"What if we don't want to?" Tanya asked. At Eric's frown, she rose. "OK. I know where I'm not wanted."

"Me, too," Sharon chimed in. "Claire, are you coming?"

"I'm not a wife. I'm exempt," she answered with a smile. "My shift at the NAB table will start soon, and I hate to waste this good food." She pointed to her plate.

"NAB table?" Dennis sounded puzzled. "What's that?"

His wife nudged him. "Non-alcoholic beverage."

"Ah," he said. Then, with a shrug, he added, "Learn something every day."

"How comforting," Sharon teased as she rose. "Claire, keep these guys in line while we're gone."

The two women left Claire at the table full of men, feeling oddly out of place. She addressed her plate of appetizers and tried to be invisible.

Eric spoke to Dennis. "Tell me the truth. If you could relive your life, would you get married again?" He blinked at his colleague then brushed off his question with one hand. "Your honeymoon isn't over yet. Forget I asked you."

He faced Mike and posed the same question. "Sure," Mike answered. "No question about it."

Eric looked at Alex. "What about you?"

Alex's gaze landed on Claire and she felt the heat she'd always felt in his presence, only several degrees hotter. "With the right woman, I wouldn't hesitate."

Somehow Claire sensed his answer wasn't hypothetical, and the thrill of knowing someone wanted her, really *wanted* her, made her toes tingle to the point where she could hardly stand to wear her shoes. In fact, her entire body tingled, and in places that hadn't tingled in years.

"Claire's widowed," Dennis said. "Why don't you get a woman's perspective?"

Eric nodded. "All right. Claire? If you'd had a horrible first marriage, would you be willing to try it again?"

Claire looked at Alex as she answered. "I don't know what I'd do if I'd had a bad experience the first time around. My marriage was wonderful, but I'd hope the second one would be just as fulfilling."

"Or in my case, just as bad."

"Whatever happened before doesn't count," she insisted. "Not only are the circumstances different, but there are two different people involved now, including yourself. You'd have a fresh slate. The fate of any marriage depends on how much each person is willing to invest in the relationship."

"Hear, hear." Mike raised his eggnog in a toast.

"So your bottom line is yes?" Dennis asked.

She should have known the men wanted a simple answer instead of her convoluted explanation.

"Without a doubt," she replied, before she noticed how the three physicians stared at her and Alex in open speculation. Suddenly embarrassed, she picked up her glass of punch and took a long drink, hoping it would cool her overheated face.

"There you have it, Eric," Alex said lightly. "The answers were unanimous. Now, if I were you, I'd pay attention to what Claire said about you being a different person in different circumstances, then call Jody and pop the question."

"First you'd better tell her what a fool you've been," Mike interjected. "Women will always forgive you if say that."

Dennis guffawed. "Is that the voice of experience talking?"

Mike grinned. "It works, so don't knock it."

"Do you love her?" Claire asked kindly, aware that if they'd been anywhere but at this party, she wouldn't have dared to pose such a personal question to a person she knew only in passing.

He didn't answer at first, then he nodded, his eyes bleak.

"Then what are you doing here?" Dennis scolded. "Go ask her to marry you and put you out of your misery."

"And if she says yes, bring her to the party and we'll have a real reason to celebrate," Alex said.

Eric rose and squared his shoulders. "All right. I'll do it."

"If I might make a suggestion," Claire offered, "I'd drink a gallon of coffee first. I doubt if she'll appreciate a proposal if she knows your courage came out of a bottle."

Mike leaned over to Alex, but spoke in a tone that everyone could hear. "By gosh, Alex. She's smart *and* gorgeous. How did you get to be so lucky?"

"Clean living," he answered promptly.

The men laughed and the somber mood that had hung over the table lifted. Eric went in search of coffee, although now that he'd made his decision he seemed more sober than he had moments earlier.

"Do you think he'll really follow through?" Claire asked on their way to relieve Nora and Roberta.

"He will," Alex said. "We could tell he loved her months ago, but he didn't admit it until now."

"I hope they're both happy."

"So do I." He stopped before they reached their destination. "Did you mean what you said about marrying again?"

"Did *you?*"

"Every word."

She nodded. "Me, too."

A broad smile appeared on his face and for the next two hours, whenever their glances met, she swore the ice in the punch bowl melted. Maybe she was crazy to feel this way so soon after she'd worked through her issues concerning Christmas, but after three years she was simply making up for lost time.

In spite of their steady stream of customers, Claire was extremely conscious of Alex's nearness. When Henry and Dianne took to the stage for the announcements and the crowd quieted, he moved in close enough for his coat to brush against her bare arm. Goose-bumps rose on her skin and she rubbed them away, certain everyone nearby could notice the sparks arcing between them.

"Cold?" he murmured in her ear.

"No," she said honestly. "Nervous."

"About the contest?"

She shook her head.

"Then what?"

Words failed her. How could she say that *he* was making her nervous by making her feel things she hadn't for a long time?

Suddenly, he gave her a feral grin. "Why, Ms Westin, am *I* making you nervous?"

"Whatever gave you that idea?" she said lightly, hoping her warm face hadn't turned pink enough for him to notice.

"I have my ways," he said. "But for the record, I'm looking forward to the end of our shift."

Anticipation shimmied down her spine. "You are? Why?"

Before he could reply, Henry gave his "Merry Christmas and Happy Holiday" speech to all the clinic staff. Then Dianne began announcing the tree contest winners. Most traditional went to Orthopedics for their old-fashioned gold balls and garlands; most whimsical went to Oncology for using every kids' meal toy supplied by fast-food restaurants; and most unusual went to the lab and radiology departments who'd joined forces and decorated their tree with test tubes, syringes, stethoscopes, old-fashioned mercury thermometers—minus the mercury—and X-ray film cut into shapes of body parts. Non-X-rated, of course.

"And the grand prize, which is given by popular vote from the entire staff," Dianne announced from the podium, "goes to…" A hush fell over the room. "Family Practice for their snowflake tree. Congratulations to Claire Westin and Alex Ridgeway."

The crowd erupted with applause and Claire stared at Alex, who appeared equally stunned. "We won?" she asked. "Did I hear her right? We won?"

He smiled. "We did."

"Oh, my." She cupped her face in her hands. "Oh, my. I can't believe it. There must be some mistake."

"I don't think so."

The band struck up and people headed for the dance floor as others congratulated them.

When the excitement died down and Dennis and his wife arrived to take over from them, Alex spoke into her ear.

"Do you know what would be a really big mistake?"

"No."

"If we don't walk onto the dance floor this minute."

"You want to dance?" Somehow he'd never struck her as the dancing type.

"Why do you think I wanted you at this party?"

"For my scintillating conversation?" she joked to hide her jitters at the notion of being nestled against him as they swayed to the music.

"Close." He held out his hand, but she hesitated, instinctively knowing that once she did, she'd officially start a new chapter. What a scary thought.

"You've come this far," he urged. "Don't stop now."

Claire couldn't go back and didn't want to stay frozen in her current state, which meant the only way to go now was forward. Slowly, uncertainly she slipped her palm against his and his warm, strong fingers closed around her own. He'd never appeared more satisfied than he did at that moment.

"That wasn't so hard, was it?" Before she could answer, he headed for the dance floor. "Come on. I don't want to waste a single note."

CHAPTER NINE

"RELAX."

Alex's gentle admonition as he drew Claire against him only made her more tense. He'd admitted to having wanted this moment for some time and she didn't want to disappoint him, but it was quite probable she would.

"A point of warning," she said. "I haven't done this for ages."

"Same here."

"I wasn't ever an Arthur Murray graduate."

"Neither was I," he said as he eased into his first steps. "But I can hold my own, so relax and don't worry about how long it's been. Dancing is like riding a bike. Once you learn, you never forget."

She stepped on his foot. "I'm not so sure about that," she apologized.

"You're entitled to have a little rust around the edges, but we'll brush it off in short order. Just feel the music and let me do the work."

She wanted to protest that she was more aware of him than the music, but as he continued to lead in a basic three-step pattern, Claire slowly found her dancing feet. By the next number she'd loosened up and before she knew it, she was floating across the floor, certain her happiness kept her feet from touching the ground.

Suit jackets and ties gradually disappeared. Men unbuttoned their collars and rolled their sleeves to their elbows while the women discarded their shawls and heels. To Claire, Alex looked devilishly handsome in his casually worn dress clothes and more often than not, she wondered if she'd walked into the middle of Cinderella's fairy-tale.

The slow tunes became her favorites and she counted the moments from the end of one to the start of another. With each, he guided her through the crowd as effortlessly as if she were a part of himself. She grew warmer as the night wore on and while his body heat was a contributing factor, her rising temperature seemed to come more from within rather than without.

When Alex led her off the dance floor and into a private side room, she followed willingly. When he pulled her back into his embrace, she went gratefully. And when he lowered his mouth to hers, she accepted him greedily.

A cleansing shower of sensations washed over her. The feel of his hard body under her hands and his unique masculine scent became indelibly marked in her mind as he trailed kisses down her neck to the hollow of her throat.

"If this is a dream…." she murmured, stopping because it took too much energy to talk.

"It isn't."

"I don't want it to end."

"It won't."

The dance number ended and she dimly heard a man announce a brief intermission.

"We'd better go back," he muttered before he captured her mouth again.

When she came up for air, she answered. "We should. Everyone will wonder where we are."

"Yeah." Alex continued to hold her and she wasn't in any hurry to leave the haven of his arms.

"What if they look for us?" she asked.

"They won't."

"You sound certain."

With Claire's head tucked under his chin, his chest rumbled with laughter and his voice carried a happy lilt. "They know better," he said. "In fact, they probably assume we took our party elsewhere."

"My purse is still at the table."

He gave a long-suffering sigh. "Women and their purses."

"Your jacket is there, too," she reminded him.

"We'll go back," he said, sounding like a little boy who was doing something under duress. "In a minute."

His kiss was infinitely tender and so full of promise that her knees buckled. He hauled her closer, until she felt every wrinkle in his trousers and every button on his shirt.

His rakish grin warmed her heart when he finally, reluctantly released her. "I should take a stroll around the building to cool off."

"We could," she suggested. "But it might be tough to explain how we both contracted pneumonia."

He laughed aloud. "That it would."

While Alex went to refill their glasses, Claire detoured to the ladies' room and could hardly believe she was the person in the mirror with rosy cheeks and sparkling eyes.

A matronly, gray-haired woman at the next basin smiled at her. "Having a good time?"

Claire blushed. "Yes."

She dug in her beaded bag and held out her compact. "You look like you could use a little of this."

"Thanks." Claire brushed a dusting of powder across her cheekbones, toning the bright rosiness to a soft glow. Nothing, however, could dim the brilliance in her eyes.

The woman patted her arm. "You look wonderful. With the lights down low, you'll look like you've simply been dancing too much."

If a complete stranger could tell she'd been thoroughly kissed, how could she face Nora and Alex's colleagues?

The woman winked. "Enjoy the rest of the evening, my dear."

Fortunately for her, Eric and Jody arrived at their table at the same time she did, effectively stealing the limelight with Eric's announcement.

"We're getting married."

"Congratulations," everyone echoed. "When's the wedding?"

"Next month," Eric answered. "And you're all invited."

The band struck up another tune and couples slowly returned to the dance floor. The final hour passed by all too quickly and soon Alex ushered Claire to the door. Between her form-fitting skirt and the high step to climb into his car, she needed a boost to get inside—a boost that he seemed quite happy to give.

"Did you have a good time?" he asked as he threaded his vehicle into the line of cars exiting the grounds.

She leaned her head against the neck rest. "The best."

"I wish I'd done one thing differently, though."

"What?"

He grinned. "Hired someone other than my mother to babysit."

To Claire, it only proved how they both were out of practice when it came to dating strategies. That wasn't necessarily a bad thing. Their relationship seemed to have progressed at light speed and it wouldn't hurt to approach the next phase with caution. "To be honest, I didn't know what to expect this evening. It turned out much better than I'd imagined."

"Hmm. I must have a more vivid imagination than you do."

"Really? You thought we'd win the grand prize and spend more time on the dance floor than anyone?"

"The prize was the icing on the cake. As for the rest, I'd hoped."

Alex may not have planned the babysitting option to accommodate the possibilities, but he'd certainly been a step ahead of her in regard to the party. She'd simply wanted to enjoy the company, the food and the music. In the end, she'd received more than she'd bargained for or dreamed possible.

"Next time, we'll plan certain aspects of the evening more carefully," he added as he reached out and held her hand in her lap.

Next time. She could hardly wait.

The sight of Alex on Monday brought Saturday night's party back into sharp focus. Instead of seeing him as he was at the moment—a physician wearing a nondescript lab coat—it was far too easy to remember him as her handsome date.

At odd times, Claire would ask Alex a professional question or clarify an order, and a lazy smile would appear on his face as if he, too, couldn't always concentrate on his work.

As the hours went by, the reality of a full patient load soon caused the weekend's memory to fade into the background.

"Did you ever return Dr Jensen's phone call?" she asked him midway through the afternoon.

He snapped his fingers. "I forgot. I'll do that right now. Who's waiting?"

"Rick Morris and Doris O'Brien. Give me a few minutes to settle them."

"I'll hurry," he promised before she called for Mrs O'Brien.

"Dr Ridgeway has to prescribe something else for my cholesterol," she said the moment she saw Claire. "Those pills I'm taking are making me sick to my stomach."

"Didn't he change your prescription the last time you came in?"

Doris nodded. "And the time before that, but I'm telling you, I'd rather die of heart disease than feel like I do now. Not only am I nauseous, but I'm exhausted all the time."

Claire scribbled her complaints on her form. "All right. He'll be in to see you shortly."

She showed Rick and his wife to the nearest room to

save him a few painful steps, but he clearly wasn't happy to be there and didn't hesitate to show it.

"I don't know why he just couldn't give me the results over the phone," he groused. "Everybody else I know talks to their doctors without having to pay for an office call."

"He must have thought it was important," Joyce commented.

Rick scoffed. "He wants to earn a living, but I can't because I'm losing an entire afternoon of work."

"Doctor thought it would be better to discuss your lab results in person," Claire said calmly, noting his blood pressure was higher than before.

"Then where the hell is he?"

"He'll be in as soon as he can." She opened the door and, as if on cue, Alex strode in.

"Good news," he said as he opened Rick's chart. "I believe we've discovered why you have that pins-and-needles feeling in your hands and feet."

Rick's sour expression turned to one of interest. "Oh, yeah?"

"According to the lab reports, you're extremely low in vitamin B12 and your red blood cells show it. In short, you have a form of anemia."

"Is that all? A few vitamins and I'll be as good as new?"

"Not quite," Alex said. "Vitamin B12 is given through injections and your deficiency is causing your neurological problems. However, giving you injections at this point wouldn't be in your best interests. We need to find out *why* your B12 level is low."

"I suppose you want to run more tests."

"A few. I also would recommend that you see a gastro-enterologist—a physician who specializes in diseases of the stomach and intestinal tract. If we don't discover the cause, we'll only be treating your symptoms."

"What are some things that could be wrong with him?" Joyce asked.

"It could be a variety of things. You see, B12 is found in meat, animal protein and legumes. The stomach has certain cells that produce what we call intrinsic factor, which is necessary to transport the vitamin through the intestine. In the majority of cases of pernicious anemia, which is what we label a vitamin B12 deficiency, the most common cause is that the stomach mucosa doesn't secrete enough of this factor to carry all of the vitamin that the body needs. As a result, you become deficient."

"So just prescribe stomach medicine," Rick said.

"Again, we need to know *why* this has happened in order to treat you properly. The problem may not even be in your stomach. It could lie in your intestine and be caused by anything from a malignancy to a tapeworm. Dietary factors might also be a consideration."

"I eat plenty of meat, so you can rule that out," Rick said.

Joyce spoke up again. "It could be cancer?"

"It's a possibility we can't ignore," Alex said.

"I'm not going to any more doctors and having any more tests. You can pad someone else's bill, but not mine." Rick folded his beefy arms across his chest. "Just start me on these shots and we'll call it good."

Alex shook his head. "I wouldn't be practicing good medicine if I didn't rule out the conditions I mentioned. What benefit would you receive if I gave you vitamin B12 and let a cancer go untreated?"

Rick rose. "It's not cancer. I'd know if it was."

"Most people don't. I would highly recommend a stomach endoscopy, at the very least."

"Sorry, Doc. You're barking up the wrong tree. I'm not going through more tests."

"These aren't painful procedures. With medication—"

"My answer's no. You can't force me to do tests I don't want."

"No, I can't."

"And I don't think I have this anemia stuff either. One of the guys at work had a pinched nerve in his back and he had the same problem."

"Our tests indicate otherwise."

"Bah! They're wrong. I'm not going for more tests and I'm certainly not coming in for shots for the rest of my life."

"The weakness in your hands and feet will only get worse," Alex warned. "Your sense of touch will become impaired, you'll lose your reflexes and will probably notice your mental state will deteriorate, too. Irritability, mild depression and paranoia may develop. But again, without the proper tests, we're only treating the symptoms and not the cause."

"We'll talk it over," Joyce interrupted.

"There's nothing to talk over. I've already decided," Rick stated in a near growl.

"If you should change your mind, call Claire and we'll set up an appointment with the specialist," Alex said.

Rick snorted. "I'm not changing my mind," he said, before he stormed from the room.

Joyce stopped at the door. "What other tests would you recommend?"

"The GI specialist will probably perform an upper GI endoscopy, a gastric analysis, a Schilling test and, quite possibly, a colonoscopy. All of those procedures can be done in either the doctor's office or as a hospital outpatient."

She nodded. "Thanks for the information. That might help."

As soon as she'd left, Claire asked, "Do you think he'll listen to her?"

"Probably not."

"I wonder why he doesn't want to know exactly what's wrong with him? Wouldn't you feel better if you knew the cause, or at least had ruled out the worst possibilities?"

"To some people, ignorance is bliss."

"I suppose. But what if we find out later he has cancer of the stomach or colon? He could sue us for malpractice."

"He could," Alex admitted, "but if he refuses my recommended treatment and I have witnesses, he won't get far. By the way, Susan Jensen found a tumor in Victor Kohls's colon. She's taking him to surgery on Thursday."

"Is it malignant?"

"She doesn't have the path report yet, but she's ninety-nine per cent certain it is."

"Poor man."

"Yeah, but if they caught it in time, he'll still have a lot of good years left."

"I'm glad. He seems like a nice old man."

He glanced at his watch, then frowned. "Is it only four o'clock?"

"Your watch has stopped *again*. When are you going to break down and buy a new one?"

"I've told you, when I find a basic, old-fashioned watch. They all have so many bells and whistles that you need a physics degree just to tell the time."

"You always say that. They aren't that bad."

"They are," he insisted. "So what time is it?"

Claire checked her own trusty watch. "A few minutes before five."

His face brightened. "Dare I hope that we've cleared out the waiting room?"

"If you saw Doris O'Brien, yes, we have."

"I took care of her before Rick."

"Did you change her cholesterol medication?"

"Yeah, but I'm running out of options."

"Could it be psychological?"

"Anything's possible, but if she doesn't want to modify

her diet then she'll have to take the tablets, even if she doesn't like the way they make her feel. That's the problem today. Everyone wants a pill so they don't have to make a lifestyle change, and the drug companies love it.''

"Now you're sounding like Rick," she teased.

Alex grinned. "I am, aren't I?" He grabbed her hands and drew her close. "How would you and Joshua like to drive around town this evening and check out the lights in the park?''

"I'd love to," she said simply.

Ten minutes before Alex and Jennie were due to arrive for their planned excursion, Claire's phone rang. Irritated by the interruption—she wanted to finish washing the dinner dishes and slip on their coats before Alex drove onto the driveway—she dried her hands and snatched up the cordless extension.

"Hello.''

"Hello, Claire. Have we caught you at a bad time?''

Recognizing the voice of Ray's mother, Marion, Claire knew this conversation would take longer than a telemarketer's spiel. Bowing to the inevitable, she softened her tone as she went to the front door to unlock it for Alex.

"Not really," she answered. "I'm trying to clear away our dinner so we can check out the lights in the park before Joshua's bedtime.''

"You're taking him to see the lights?" Marion's voice was cool.

Aware of Marion's views about Christmas, Claire minimized their upcoming excursion. "The children at his sitter's are always talking about the park display, so I thought it would be a nice outing for us. Regardless, it's always good to hear from you. How is Leroy?''

Her ploy to change the subject worked because Marion replied with, "The usual aches and pains from growing older. How's my grandson?''

Claire glanced through the doorway to see Joshua happily dividing his attention between his cars and the twinkling lights of their tree. "Great. He's really enjoying our tree."

The pregnant pause made her realize her second mistake.

"You have a *Christmas* tree?"

The horror in her mother-in-law's voice was obvious. "It's just a small one," Claire hurried to explain. "A friend gave it to us. Actually, he gave it to Joshua."

"Humph." Marion's disgust came through clearly over the phone line. "If you have a tree, I suppose you've been jumping into all of the holiday fanfare, too."

The guilt Claire had put behind her now struck with full force under Marion's scathing tone, but she struggled to hold it at bay as she returned to the kitchen. Tucking the phone under one ear, she returned to her dishes. "A small tree and one office party doesn't mean a lot of fanfare."

"How you can party during this time of year is beyond me. Have you forgotten Ray to the point that you can *celebrate* so soon after his death?"

She forced her voice to sound even. "It's been three years, Marion. Josh's entire lifetime." She didn't realize until she'd spoken that she'd used Alex's nickname for her son. "As I said earlier, one office gathering can't be considered a celebration."

"Humph."

Although she knew she'd never convince Marion otherwise, she felt compelled to try. "Christmas isn't about Ray or his death. It's about something much bigger."

"Well," Marion retorted, "if that's the way you feel, then fine. If you want to forget Ray, go ahead, but I never thought I'd see this day with my own two eyes. How my son's own wife could do such a thing is beyond my comprehension."

Tears burned Claire's throat and a pang shot through in

her chest. All thoughts of dishes in the cooling water faded and she abandoned them to soak. "I won't forget Ray," she said flatly as she sank onto a kitchen chair. "Ever. How could I?"

Movement in one corner of her eye caught her attention and she was horrified to see Alex standing silently in the doorway, his expression impassive.

Never had she felt the clash between her old life and her new one so strongly.

"I don't suppose there's any point in inviting you and Joshua to join us at our annual weekend getaway," Marion continued in her sharp tone.

For the last two years they'd holed up at their cabin on the lake to avoid partaking in the season. Claire had gone with them the first year, but last year she'd volunteered for the Christmas Day shift at the hospital and hadn't.

"No, Marion," Claire said softly, "we're going to stay here. Give our love to Leroy."

Conscious of Alex's unrelenting stare, she disconnected the call. "My mother-in-law," she explained. "This is a hard time of year for her."

He nodded. "I see. And now you're feeling guilty."

It was so unfair that he could read her so well. She studied the buttons on her phone. "A little, yes."

"I think it's more than a little."

She met his gaze. "I don't want or *like* to feel this way."

"But you do."

Claire hesitated. "Yes."

"Do you regret Saturday night?" His tension was obvious in his voice, as if he hated to ask the question but couldn't prevent himself.

How could she regret the best thing that had happened to her since Joshua's birth? "Part of me does," she said, hating to see his face take on a stony appearance, "and part of me doesn't. The problem is, I don't know what to think or do or feel.'' She pinched the bridge of her nose. ''I've never been so confused over something in my life.''

''We can see the lights tomorrow—'' Alex began.

Shaking her head, she rose. ''No. I want to go—now. I *need* this.'' Maybe a few hours with Alex would help her regain the equilibrium that Marion had destroyed in a few short minutes.

''Good girl.''

But try as she may, Claire couldn't forget Marion's accusation as they drove through the park. The elaborate light displays passed by in a haze of sameness as her mind raced to find answers to the questions she'd thought she'd put behind her.

How could she possibly enjoy herself knowing that Ray's parents were still suffering? And how could she possibly think of a rosy future for herself as she approached another anniversary of Ray's death?

An hour and a half later, as Alex carried a tired Joshua into her house, once more guilt had landed on her doorstep.

''I'm sorry for being such lousy company,'' she told him as he set Joshua on his feet. ''I didn't mean to ruin your evening.''

He smiled, although she noticed that it didn't reach his eyes. ''We saw the lights, the kids were delighted, and I was able to spend time with you. That isn't a ruined evening.''

She shrugged, not convinced.

''After a decent night's sleep, you'll put everything back into perspective. You've come too far to turn back now. Remember that.''

She nodded, hoping he was right.

Alex tried to follow the advice he'd given Claire—to get a good night's sleep—but he found it impossible. Her brittle smile and over-bright eyes haunted him and he knew that her mother-in-law's conversation had replanted the doubt she'd uprooted only a short time ago. Unfortunately, he couldn't ask Eddie for a few more words of wisdom.

He was on his own.

At least Claire was here, with him and not with the people who so clearly didn't want her to move ahead with her life. All he had to do was carry on as usual and Claire would see that she'd made the right decision to go forward.

Wouldn't she?

But as the next few days slid past and Claire missed their regular Wednesday lunch, Alex's own fears began to grow. Perhaps she hadn't gotten over Ray after all. If that was the case, where did that leave him? And how could he compete with a memory?

On Friday, Nora cornered Claire in the small lab which doubled as her office. "What's with the sad face all week?"

Claire avoided her gaze. "What sad face?"

Nora snorted. "You know what I mean. You've moped for the last four days and I want to know why. Alex doesn't look much better." Her eyes narrowed. "Did the two of you fight?"

"No." Claire was aghast. "Absolutely not."

"Then what is going on between you two? And don't tell me it's my imagination because I've fielded questions from other people. People who were at the party, I might add, and saw the way you two looked at each other."

Claire sank onto a stool and rested one elbow on the counter behind her. "Ray's mother called."

"I might have known." Nora's disgust was obvious. "And she said things like 'How could you forget my son?' and 'How dare you enjoy yourself at this time of year?' Right?"

Claire stared at her friend in surprise. "How did you guess?"

"This isn't molecular science. It's a case of two people

who are still mourning their son and they expect everyone else to do the same. Especially you.''

With the subject out in the open, Claire couldn't contain herself. Her thoughts had run in circles until she didn't know up from down, right from wrong.

''She made me feel so guilty because I had a tree in my house and went to the office party. I shudder to think what she would have said if I'd mentioned Alex.''

Nora sank onto a chair. ''How *do* you feel about Alex?''

How could she answer? Those feelings had turned her inside out for the past four days. ''I really want him in my life and Joshua's,'' she said slowly, ''but—''

''There are no buts,'' Nora said firmly. ''Your memories of Ray won't keep you warm at night or make your toes tingle. Need I remind you that you already went down this road before the party?''

''I know, and I thought I'd gotten over the worst, but Marion and Leroy are having such a difficult time. It doesn't seem right that I should be happy when they're not.''

''It's their choice,'' Nora said firmly. ''You've gone to the next phase of your grief—acceptance—and they haven't, but that's their problem, not yours. You can't let them hold you back. Why do you think I was so insistent you move away from them and come here? I knew if you stayed close to their influence, you'd wear widow's weeds the rest of your life. And that would be a waste.''

''Joshua and I would have a good life together,'' she insisted.

''Of course you would, but with Alex, wouldn't it be so much better? What about those three children you always wanted? Are you willing to settle for less because two people don't want you to go after what makes you happy?''

No, she didn't. Neither could she deny the truth—Alex

made her feel complete. "It would have been so much simpler if this wasn't happening now, at Christmas."

"Did you ever stop to think that this was the *perfect* time of year for you?"

Claire stared at Nora. "You're kidding, right?"

Nora shrugged. "It seems strangely appropriate in a cosmic sense. Alex is a mighty fine gift to be receiving right now."

She hadn't thought of it in those terms, but Nora could be right. Whether one called it fate, or Ray's way of looking out for her from the Great Beyond, Alex's arrival in her life was truly a gift. With that realization came the knowledge of what she had to do next.

"I'm afraid I hurt his feelings," she said, thinking of his mood of late. Oh, he'd been kind and polite but somewhat distant, as if he'd been preparing himself for bad news. "He hasn't said two words to me that weren't work-related."

Nora shrugged. "Can you blame him? He has his pride. I've heard that he practically begged his ex to work on their marriage, but she left anyway. He's simply waiting for your move, so talk to him. If you don't, he'll think the worst, if he doesn't already."

Claire glanced at her watch. "Our afternoon patients will arrive soon. I won't have enough time."

"Oh, rubbish." Nora rose and dragged Claire off her stool. "You, my dear, have already wasted four days. Why wait a minute longer?" She shoved her toward the door. "Go on. He's in his office."

Claire looked at Nora over her shoulder. "And what are you going to do?"

Nora grinned. "What every good friend does. I'll watch your back and keep the wolves at bay until you two straighten yourselves out."

"Wish me luck?"

"And then some. Now, hurry up." Nora nudged Claire forward. "The suspense is killing me."

Claire drew a deep breath before she knocked on Alex's door and poked her head inside. It pained her to see the harsh lines on his face where she'd once seen laugh lines, but perhaps, after the next few minutes, she would again.

"Hi," she said brightly. "Do you have a few minutes?"

He leaned back in his chair and tossed his pen onto a stack of papers. Wariness replaced his initial curiosity and she hated that she'd caused him such obvious grief.

"For you, of course," he said smoothly.

She stepped inside, suddenly nervous. "Do you remember when you asked me if I regretted our night at the party?"

"Yes." His voice sounded cautious.

"And do you remember how I said that I didn't know?"

Alex nodded.

"Well, I just wanted to tell you that I didn't regret a single moment of that night and I don't now." She brushed a lock of hair off her forehead. "I never did, but my mother-in-law's phone call threw me for a loop. It took me a while to straighten everything out in my own mind, but I have."

"I see." He held his index fingers to his mouth.

The few seconds of silence were deafening and Claire's determination—and hopes—faded. "Anyway, I just thought you should know."

She headed for the door, but before she could reach it, Alex's arm barred the opening. His breath caressed the back of her neck and she shivered.

"Did you just say what I think you said?" he asked, his mouth hovering over her ear.

Her heart had somehow leapt into her throat and she couldn't speak. Instead, she nodded.

"The question is, will I have to compete with Ray's memory?"

She twisted herself around to face him. ''No. I'll always remember him, because Joshua is his son and will want to know the kind of man his father was, but I'm ready for a new chapter.''

Before she realized it, she was in his arms and his mouth was against hers in an emotionally charged kiss that would have cut her off at the knees if he hadn't been holding her. She was so happy, she could have sworn that she was soaring, but the feel of her hands on his back as she traced every muscle kept her rooted to the ground.

''You're certain,'' he muttered against her mouth.

''One…hundred…and…ten…per…cent.'' As his lips traveled down her neck in a trail of fire, she could hardly breathe. ''Oh, Alex.''

''Ahem.''

The distinct sound of someone clearing their throat in the hallway managed to penetrate the sensual fog surrounding her. She and Alex broke apart to see Nora wearing a huge smile on her face.

''If you two have worked things out, and from the smoke coming out of this room I'd say you have, I'm afraid duty calls. Roberta is about to do her caged-tiger imitation.''

Alex released her, but the warm glow residing inside her made up for the loss. ''I'll be right there,'' Claire said.

Nora gave a jaunty salute before she headed down the hall, presumably to her own tasks.

Alex stared at Claire with hungry eyes. ''Did you know you have lousy timing?''

''Not until I met you,'' she replied with a smile.

He stroked her cheek. ''I don't know if I can concentrate on medicine instead of you for the next few hours.''

Thinking of the weekend ahead and what might transpire, she nodded. ''Then we're both in the same boat, Dr Ridgeway.''

*   *   *

The weekend turned out as wonderfully as Claire had imagined. She and Joshua spent nearly the entire time with Alex and Jennie, and she and Alex were fortunate enough to steal a private hour here and there. By the time Monday rolled around, she was sorry to have to share him with his patients once again.

"What should we do this evening?" Alex asked her. "Take Joshua to see Santa Claus at the mall?"

Claire shook her head. "Christmas is only a week away and I have a few more gifts to find."

"Would you like us to watch Josh for you?"

"Thanks, but Nora's already volunteered. We're still on for tomorrow night, though, aren't we?"

"Yeah. Jennie's talked about it all weekend. She can't wait for the annual network showing of *Rudolph*. I think that's her favorite Christmas cartoon."

"Mine, too." Knowing of his daughter's love for popcorn, Claire planned to have plenty on hand. To make the treat more special for their movie night, she'd serve it in her plastic boxes that were identical to the paper ones used at the theaters.

"And don't forget her pageant is on Wednesday night."

"As if I could." Jennie had marked Claire's calendar with a huge red X. "I'm looking forward to it."

He pulled her closer. "Are you sure you don't need company while you're shopping?"

"Some things are best done alone," she said lightly. She'd finally gotten an idea for his gift and she didn't want him tagging along.

"Dr Ridgeway." Roberta's voice came over the intercom. "Phone call on line two."

Alex planted a swift kiss on her mouth. "Have fun."

"Shopping for presents is hard work, not fun," she corrected.

"Then don't work too hard."

"I'll try."

Although Claire knew what she wanted to buy, finding it proved difficult. After visiting several jewelry stores, she was about to give up, but one little shop tucked at the end of the block, off the beaten path, caught her eye.

To her great relief, they carried the exact watch she'd been looking for. "Most men want something a little more high-tech," the jeweler said, "but we have a few who don't."

Claire gave a cursory glance at the tray of watches that had more dials on their face than the cockpit of a 747 before she studied the one in her hand. "This one is perfect."

"Would you like us to wrap it for you?"

"Thanks, but I'll do it myself."

With this major purchase under her belt, she drove to the Super-Mart. Fortunately for her bank account, the small starter sewing machine she wanted for Jennie was on sale. It was only capable of straight and zigzag stitching, but Claire knew the youngster would be thrilled. Her interest in sewing had been obvious during their hours of working together on Jennie's costume and Claire knew that with Jennie's creativity and her eye for color, she would want to sew all sorts of things in the future.

Pleased with her success, she stood in the checkout line and was surprised when Edwina and Joe joined her.

"You're shopping, too, I see," Claire said cheerfully as the clerk rang up her purchase.

Edwina appeared pale and her smile seemed forced. "Finishing up the last few things on my list. You?"

Claire motioned to the box now enclosed in a sack. "Same here."

"I can't say I won't be glad to stay at home," Eddie said as she rubbed her stomach. "It gets crazier every year." Without warning, she gasped and bent over.

Joe grabbed her arm. "What's wrong?"

Eddie moaned. "The baby."

CHAPTER TEN

CLAIRE had seen a lot of expectant fathers, but none wore the look of sheer terror that Joe did.

"Oh, my gosh," he said, horrified. "Why didn't you say something before now?"

"Because it just hit me."

"Let's find a place for you to sit down," Claire said. "Joe, finish your business and I'll look after her." Without waiting for his agreement, she grabbed Eddie's arm with one hand. With the other pushing her cart, she led her to the restored foyer where management had thoughtfully provided benches for tired shoppers.

Claire helped Eddie sit on a bench before she took her pulse. It was fast, which wasn't surprising. "How are you doing?"

"Not so good." She gripped Claire's hand hard enough to leave bruises. "I haven't felt right all day, and I couldn't put my finger on it, but now...something's definitely wrong. I thought contractions were supposed to come and go."

"You're having one long steady pain?"

Eddie bit her lip and nodded. "It's easing now, but it reminds me of the last time."

The last time being her miscarriage. Claire placed her free hand on Eddie's uterus and felt what seemed like spasmodic twitching rather than a muscle contraction.

"Here's what we'll do," she said, patting her hand. "You're going to lie down while I call for an ambulance. I think your baby is ready to make his or her appearance."

"Can't Joe drive me?"

"He could, but the paramedics can start an IV and save

148

time." She glanced up and saw Joe approach with a worried frown on his face. "Here he is, so I'll go—"

Eddie didn't release her hand. "Stay," she begged. "Please?"

Keeping her patient calm was paramount. If having a nurse nearby helped, Claire wouldn't leave. She turned to Joe. "Go back inside and ask the ladies at the service desk to call for an ambulance." Because she'd seen a small but definite red stain on Edwina's trousers, she added, "Ask for a blanket, too."

He obeyed without argument. "Now, Eddie, I need both hands," she said kindly. "I want to call Dr Ridgeway so he can meet you at the hospital."

Eddie nodded.

Claire's fingers were numb from Eddie's death grip, but she pulled off her coat and covered Eddie before she managed to punch the numbers into her cellphone. "Please, be home," she murmured under her breath, relieved when he was.

"It's Claire," she announced without preamble. Turning her back to her patient, she lowered her voice. "Edwina Butler is with me at the Super-Mart and she's having problems. Her uterus is tender and I can feel mild muscle spasms. She appears comfortable for the moment, but she's also bleeding."

"How much?"

"It doesn't seem severe, but I can't tell for certain. We've called for an ambulance."

"I'm on my way to the hospital."

"Do you want me to call ahead for you?"

"I'll do it," he said. "If her placenta is tearing, I want Jivanta and the surgical team ready to roll."

Jivanta was one of the obstetricians who was often teased because she wasn't much larger than the infants she delivered. She might come in a small package, but she specialized in high-risk pregnancies and often lived up to her name which meant "gives life." Eddie would be in excellent hands.

"I'll tell her."

She rang off and smiled brightly at Eddie and Joe, who'd just returned with the manager and a blanket.

"Is there anything I can do?" the man she recognized from the accident at the store a few weeks earlier asked.

Claire smiled at him. "Clear the area for the ambulance crew."

While he and one of his assistants did as she'd instructed, Claire explained the situation to the couple. "Dr Ridgeway is going to meet us at the hospital."

"I'm losing the baby, aren't I?"

"There's a possibility you'll need a C-section if the baby's in distress," Claire explained, "but they'll do everything they can for both of you."

"They have to save my baby. They *have* to. I can't go through it again."

"I know," Claire said, feeling the woman's pain more acutely than Eddie would ever know. "It's important for you to relax. Take normal breaths." A distant wail slowly increased in volume and she could see flashing lights approach.

"Just a few more minutes and you'll be on your way," she told Eddie. "How's the pain?"

"I feel pretty good now that I'm lying down."

The ambulance careened to a stop in front of the door and Claire quickly briefed them on the situation. While one paramedic took Eddie's vital signs and listened for the baby's heartbeat, the other started an IV.

As soon as they'd done all they could, they bundled her onto a stretcher and headed for the hospital.

"Will you come with me?" Joe asked. "It would mean a lot to us if you were there. At least until we know if...if..." His voice choked and Claire's eyes filled with moisture.

She didn't want to feel Eddie's and Joe's anguish if Alex couldn't save their baby, but she couldn't refuse Joe's request.

"I'll follow in my car," she promised.

By the time she and Joe arrived, Alex and Jivanta were already attending to Eddie. Several minutes later, nurses wheeled Eddie to surgery and Alex stopped to talk to Joe.

"The baby's in distress," he said. "We're running out of time."

"Will he…will he make it?" Joe asked.

"We'll do our best. The good news is, their condition isn't as bad as it could be."

"What went wrong?"

"Part of Eddie's placenta is tearing away from her uterus, and that means the baby is losing blood and not getting all the oxygen he needs."

"Once he's born, he'll be OK?" Joe asked.

"We'll do everything we can," Alex answered. "I'll find you when we're done." With that parting remark, he hurried toward the surgical suites.

"Would you like to call someone?" Claire asked Joe. "Your parents?"

He shook his head. "I'd rather wait until it's over. One way or another." His voice was flat, as if he didn't dare hope for a positive outcome. "If she loses this baby, she won't pull through. I'll lose her, too."

Claire understood, but couldn't find the words of encouragement he so desperately needed. Telling him to think positively and hope for the best seemed trite. Fate didn't always listen to positive thoughts or fulfill desperate hopes.

"Would you mind staying a little longer?" he asked. "I know you have your own family…"

Aware of how waiting was the worst and waiting alone made it even more so, she simply couldn't desert him. "I

just need to let Josh's sitter know I'll be late. In the meantime, how about a cup of coffee?''

By the time she'd explained the situation to Nora and
their coffee had cooled, Alex had reappeared in his surgical scrubs.

''Congratulations, Joe. You have a beautiful little girl.''

Joe's mouth dropped open. ''I do?''

''Five pounds seven ounces.''

''Is she…is she OK?''

''She's struggling a bit right now, so you won't be able
to hold her. We want to make sure her oxygen level stays
where it should. She lost some blood, so we're replacing
it.''

''And Eddie?'' he asked.

''Eddie's fine. She had what we call a grade one sepa-
ration, which means that less than ten per cent of the placenta became detached. It's too soon to tell what—if any—
problems your daughter might have, but her Apgar scores
aren't bad, considering what she's been through.''

''Can I see both of them?'' Joe asked.

''Eddie's on her way to Recovery, but you might catch
a glimpse of your baby through the nursery window. Our
pediatrician, Dr Tuttle, intends to airlift her to a neonatal
center within the hour, though. They're more equipped to
handle situations like this than we are but, honestly, everyone is optimistic.''

Joe enthusiastically pumped Alex's hand up and down.
''Thank you, Doctor. For everything. I guess I have a few
phone calls to make, don't I?'' He hurried off to the desk
in the corner where a telephone was available.

''They're both going to be OK?''

Alex smiled at her. ''I'd say so. Tuttle will want to be
on the safe side, and I can't blame him.''

''I'm glad. All I could think of was how devastated
Eddie would be if things went wrong at this stage of the
game. Do you know when it might have happened?''

"Relatively recently. Maybe even while she was shopping. If so, it was probably a good thing."

"Why?"

"She said after the initial pain, it wasn't so bad. She might have dismissed it until the situation got out of hand." He paused. "This wasn't easy for you, was it?"

Claire shrugged, minimizing her own bad memories. "I managed."

"You didn't have to stay."

"Joe asked me to," she said simply. "Even if he hadn't, I couldn't leave without knowing. One way or the other."

Alex touched the side of her face. "I would have called you."

"Yeah, but for some things, I'm rather short on patience."

"I'll file that away for future reference," he teased. "Does this mean I can't put your present under the Christmas tree until December 24th?"

His thoughtfulness in buying her a gift filled an empty spot in her heart. "If it's under your tree and not mine, I can survive the suspense."

"Then I'm glad we're coming to your house tomorrow night instead of mine," he said. "I'd hate to treat you like I treat Jennie. Any sniffing around the packages results in waiting an extra day to open them. One year, she wasn't supposed to unwrap hers until December 26th."

"You didn't make her wait, did you?"

He chuckled. "Actually, we only postponed the excitement until after breakfast on Christmas Day."

She poked his hard chest. "I knew it. Underneath that tough exterior is an old softy."

"Yeah, well, don't tell anyone. Especially Jennie because, believe it or not, she learned her lesson." Suddenly, he pulled her into the vacant hallway to kiss her. "I'll call you later."

"I'll be home," she promised. He wouldn't phone until

after Josh was in bed, but she'd count the minutes until then.

She watched him stride confidently down the corridor. He'd brought so many changes in her life, *good* changes that she might never have seen if she hadn't moved to Pleasant Valley. He and his daughter had helped her in ways they would probably never fully realize.

One thing she did know, however. Without a conscious effort on her part, the most surprising thing had taken place.

She'd fallen in love.

Alex returned to the OR changing rooms, his spirits as high as the kites he'd flown as a boy. Not only could he celebrate with the Butlers—some cases of abruptio placentae didn't end on such a positive note—but the fact that Claire had stuck by Joe when she could have gone about her business impressed him mightily.

He knew it had been tough for her to wait for news that could have been bad. No doubt, she'd probably relived her own sad memories, yet she hadn't run away.

She hadn't run away. Suddenly, he realized it was the one standard by which he subconsciously judged the women he dated. The truth was, there had been several opportunities for Claire to take the easy way out and leave without a backward glance—the episode with her mother-in-law had been one of the most recent—but she hadn't. Until Claire had successfully ridden this latest emotional roller-coaster, he hadn't known he'd been bracing himself for her to follow in his ex-wife's footsteps.

He'd almost given up hope of finding a woman who would stand by him through thick and thin, who possessed enough strength of character to place someone else's needs above her own, but he'd found her in Claire. He wasn't going to let the woman he loved slip through his fingers.

He wasn't the only one who thought she was a gem.

His mother thought she was wonderful and Jennie sang her praises. Claire had become such a part of his life that he couldn't imagine passing a day without hearing her voice or seeing her smile.

Claire had gone Christmas shopping tonight. He didn't know if she'd found what she'd been looking for, but he knew exactly what he wanted—no, *needed*—to buy before the stores closed for the holiday—something that would change his life and the lives of three others forever.

"Who brought cookies today?" Alex asked as he walked into the staff lounge adjoining the receptionist's office.

Claire popped her last bite into her mouth. "Nora. I was going to indulge later, but they looked delicious, especially on an empty stomach."

"Skipped breakfast?"

"I overslept," she explained. "Joshua didn't sleep well. He had a bit of a tummyache, but he's fine this morning. How's Eddie and the baby?"

"The baby's stable and Eddie's indulging herself with chocolates. After Jivanta discharges her tomorrow, they plan to visit little Miss Butler."

"Did they decide on a name?" As of last night, they hadn't chosen one for fear of jinxing Eddie's pregnancy.

He grinned. "Alexis Claire."

"Oh, my gosh. Are you serious?"

"As serious as a heart attack," he said. "They're going to call her Lexie."

"No one's ever named their child after me before."

"Same here."

"You mean there aren't a lot of Alexanders and Alexises in the world because of you?"

"Not a one. Until now. I obviously don't leave a lasting impression on my pregnant patients."

Claire privately disagreed.

"Say," he asked, "did you finish your shopping last night?"

"And my wrapping. Everything's under the tree, so now I can kick back and relax while the rest of the world spends the next few days rushing around for their last-minute gifts."

"Lucky you."

"I was wondering…would you and Jennie like to come early tonight and share our pot of beef stew? For some reason, I can't make a small batch. I tend to add a little of everything, and before I know it, I have enough to feed a platoon."

"You don't need to offer twice. What time?"

"Whenever. The stew and I are flexible."

"How about six?"

That would give her about an hour to hurry home, open her mail and change her clothes. "Six is great."

For the rest of the morning, nothing could dampen Claire's good mood. Nothing, that was, until Joyce Morris appeared in the waiting room.

Claire ushered her to an exam cubicle, noticing how she cradled her right wrist.

"I think it's sprained," Joyce said as she held it out for Claire to see.

The joint was swollen and purplish and Claire winced sympathetically. "How did it happen?"

"I tripped and fell on it," she said.

"Doctor will want X-rays."

"I guessed as much."

"Let me do my usual, and then I'll check with him." Claire pushed up the woman's sleeve to take her blood pressure and saw five black marks around her upper arm, as if someone had held her in a bruising grip. She didn't comment on their presence, but intended to tell Alex about them when she saw him.

As soon as she'd finished, she hunted him down and reported her observation. "I don't think she fell at all."

His gaze grew intent. "You don't know that for sure."

"No, but I'm right. Deep down, I'm positive."

He let out a long breath. "It wouldn't surprise me, but if she won't admit it, there's nothing we can do. Send her to the clinic radiology department and put a rush on those films. Maybe those will tell us something."

Thirty minutes later, the technician delivered the X-rays. Alex slid them onto his view box and whistled. "I hate it when my patients don't tell the truth."

"She didn't fall?"

"She may have fallen, but she didn't break her arm when she did. She has an oblique fracture."

"Doesn't a twisting motion cause that?"

"Usually."

Claire followed him into Joyce's room and stood in the background while he greeted her with his normal equanimity.

"It's broken, Joyce," he told her.

She brushed at her red-rimmed eyes. "Sorry. My arm hurts like the dickens. Are you sure it isn't a bad sprain?"

"The bone's broken," he said firmly.

She squared her shoulders. "Can you slap on a cast and send me on my way?"

"You have an oblique fracture, which means the bone snapped when it was being twisted. Aligning those edges is a little more tricky than if it was a clean break. I'll call Dr Wheatley and arrange for him to see you."

"Can't you just splint it for now?"

"The bone has to be set so it will grow straight," Alex said. "Splinting is only a temporary fix."

"Can't you do it?"

He paused to look over Joyce's head at Claire. "I could, but it would take longer for me to do the job than Dr

Wheatley. He does this sort of thing all the time. Wouldn't you rather allow a specialist to do the honors?''

"I'd rather have you," she said stubbornly.

He hesitated, and Claire mentally urged him to do the job. He was fully capable, although she understood why the physicians referred orthopedic cases. Like anything else, setting bones wasn't always as easy as it sounded.

"All right, but after I give you something for the pain, you can't drive."

Joyce nodded. "My brother is using my van. I'm supposed to call him when I'm finished."

Claire retrieved the necessary supplies while Alex left to study the X-rays again. When he returned, Claire had everything laid out and he started to work.

"Want to tell us what happened?" he asked as they waited for the painkiller to take hold.

Joyce pinched the bridge of her nose and her voice sounded dull. "Rick and I got into a fight. He won't come back for more tests because he's convinced he has a pinched nerve. He made an appointment with a chiropractor.

"I told him he wouldn't get better, just like you said," she continued, "but he got mad and wouldn't listen." She swiped her eyes and Claire handed her a facial tissue.

"So he grabbed you," Alex supplied.

"Not then. I said if he wouldn't take care of himself and make sure he didn't have cancer, I would leave. I'd put up with enough from him and if he wanted to die slowly or become completely helpless, I wasn't going to stick around and watch. That's when he got upset and grabbed me. I was trying to get away when this happened."

"Did he realize you were hurt?" Claire asked.

"I don't think so."

She stared at Alex, then at Claire. "Rick is working out of town for the next two days on a job site and won't be back until tomorrow night. I intend to move out before he gets home. My mother and Wendy are at my place now with my brother, packing up as much as they can, but I want to be sure they only load our stuff. I don't want Rick claiming I stole his things.''

"Have you taken any legal action? Asked for a restraining order?" Alex asked.

"No. Should I?"

"It would be for your protection. And Wendy's," Claire added.

"When should I do that?" She rubbed her injured arm.

"As soon as we set your arm, we'll call our staff social worker. I'm sure she can manage something at her end."

"I hate to cause everyone all this trouble," Joyce began.

"We're here to help," Alex told her.

Joyce's eyes brimmed with tears. "You don't know what this means to me."

Claire hugged her. "I think we do. Now, try to relax," she said as she slipped the stocking-like sleeve over Joyce's arm to protect her skin. "If it helps not to watch, then don't."

Joyce obediently closed her eyes and Alex maneuvered the edges into place. "I'm going to splint this so we can take another X-ray. If the bone is aligned, we'll add the cast."

Claire escorted Joyce back to Radiology and when they'd taken the required pictures, she escorted her back with the new set of films.

Satisfied with his efforts, Alex quickly wrapped the pre-plastered strips around her arm before they hardened. After he'd finished, he said, "If you notice your fingers swelling or if the cast feels tight, come back immediately. Otherwise, I'll see you in about six weeks."

Claire slipped away to call Paula Tucker, the social worker, and privately brief her on Joyce's situation. When she'd ended the conversation, she walked Joyce to Paula's office and left her in the other woman's care.

"Good idea to take her there yourself," Alex said when she returned.

"I didn't think you'd mind if I slipped away. I was afraid she'd have second thoughts."

"I was afraid of that, too. With luck, Joyce and Wendy will be gone before Rick realizes she's left him."

Claire nodded. "I can't understand how he could believe his co-worker's diagnosis instead of a physician's. A pinched nerve?"

"I'm not discounting the work a chiropractor does, but in his case a spinal adjustment won't help," Alex stated.

"Once he realizes that, maybe he'll come back."

"Let's hope it won't be too late."

Alex received word later in the day that young Lexie Butler was doing well and staying at the neonatal center for observation. Victor Kohls's surgery showed the tumor hadn't spread outside his intestine and Dr Jensen was satisfied that she'd removed it in its entirety. He'd need some chemotherapy to make sure the cancer didn't return, but the prognosis was excellent.

The social worker had taken Joyce in hand and had set the legal ball rolling for her. Alex hoped that Rick would deal with his wife's leaving far better than he did with his health problems.

All in all it had been an eventful day, and at Claire's house later, Alex was more than ready to sit back and shelve his patients' problems in the back of his mind. Good food and good company were the two things he wanted and at the moment he had them both.

"Your stew was delicious," he told Claire as he helped her rinse the bowls and stow them in the dishwasher.

"Thanks. Would you like to take some home? There's more than enough."

"I'd love to. You weren't kidding when you said you made enough for an army."

"Now you know why I don't make stew very often. I can't tell when to stop adding vegetables. I usually only fix it when I know I'll have a crowd, like when my family comes to visit."

"Are they coming for Christmas?"

"No. My brother is a fireman and has to work over the holiday. My mother was going to visit us, but her sister had a stroke and Mom thinks it might be the last time she'll see her so she's flying to Oregon. With Christmas falling on a Sunday and our office closed on Monday, we'll have a quiet, three-day weekend."

"Then you have to join us," he informed her. "My mother won't mind."

"I'd like that," she said.

Tell her what else you'd like.

Alex's courage faltered, but he decided to risk it.

"There's something you should know," he said as he carried more dirty dishes from the table to the sink.

"What's that?"

He leaned across her to shut off the faucet. Right or wrong, he wanted her full attention.

"I realize we've moved rather fast in our relationship," he said, "but for me, what we have is downright exceptional."

Claire's eyes seemed to melt. "It is for me, too."

"Neither of us are ready to rush into anything, but I'm thinking along permanent lines, like combining households."

She hesitated. "Are you asking—?"

"For you to consider marrying me," he said. "Like I said before, things have moved fast and we both need time, but I wanted you to know how I feel and the direction I'm heading. I love you, Claire, and I want us to be together all the time."

"Oh, Alex. I'd like that, too."

He smiled at her, aware that it held both happiness and relief, and drew her close. "I'm glad we're on the same wavelength."

He bent his head and kissed her with one of the long, leisurely kisses that he saved for their moments alone. She snuggled against him and the clock stood still as she opened her mouth to him.

Another step and he had her right where he wanted her, trapped at the counter with no place to go but through him. An urge to have that happen, where two became one, grew stronger as he delighted in the little moans of pleasure coming from her throat.

Cradling the back of her head in his palm, he anchored her to him and poured every thought, every feeling he had for this woman into his kiss. She responded in kind and he could hardly believe his good fortune.

He wanted to make love with her, here and now, but the kitchen table wasn't the place to make a first-time memory. Later, he thought as he explored every hill and valley until he'd drawn his own private, mental map of her body.

He was soaring above the earth, ready to explode in a shower of sparks that rivaled a fireworks display. This went beyond his wildest imagination, but he didn't want it to stop. He wanted it to last forever, and he intended to enjoy every minute, every second. He was—

"Daddy! You're *kissing* Claire." The accusation in Jennie's voice brought him back to earth with a nasty thump.

He straightened, keeping Claire in the circle of his arms. He refused to act guiltily or pretend his feelings weren't as serious or as honorable as they were. "Yes, I was," he said calmly.

"You can't do that," she protested.

"Why not?"

"Because. Because she's a *friend.*"

Alex hugged Claire and smiled at her before he addressed his daughter. "Yes, she is, but she's more than that."

Jennie's eyes narrowed. "You're not going to *marry* her, are you?"

"I want to," he answered.

"But, Daddy," Jennie wailed, "we don't need her. We're fine the way we are."

"Yes, but think how nice it would be to live together in the same house."

Jennie stomped her feet. "No. I won't do it. You promised." She glared at Claire. "You tricked me. You only pretended to be my friend. You're like the others. You just want my dad for yourself."

Claire stepped forward. "That's not true, Jennie."

"Yes, it is," she shouted, backing away. "I don't want you in my house and I don't want to be in yours." With that, she burst into tears and ran from the room.

"I apologize," Alex said. "I don't know what's come over her. She loves you and Josh."

"You're changing her life without her permission," Claire said simply. "Naturally, she'll be upset."

"Being upset is one thing. Being rude is another." A distant door slammed and he frowned. "What was that?"

Claire's eyes were filled with concern. "You don't suppose she decided to walk home, do you?"

"Better home than someplace else," he said grimly.

He rushed into the living room and peered through the window, cursing because it was too dark to see beyond Claire's yard. Immediately he strode to the closet and shoved hangers aside as he half listened to Claire's and Joshua's conversation.

"Where's Jennie?" she asked.

"'Ennie went bye."

Josh's comment only confirmed what he didn't see

hanging in the closet. He grabbed his own jacket. "Her coat's gone. I'd better go after her."

Claire followed him to the door. "You'll call, so I'll know she's safe and sound?"

"I will." He kissed her quickly. "Don't worry. I'll talk to her and everything will be fine."

She nodded.

Alex hurried outside. Not seeing a familiar form illuminated by the streetlamp, he cursed once again and slid behind the wheel of his vehicle. He hardly breathed until he saw Jennie trudging up the driveway of their house, her chin tucked against her chest.

"Thank you," he breathed softly. He'd received one miracle, and now he had to work on making another.

"How's Jennie?" Claire asked Alex on Wednesday morning.

He shook his head, appearing as disgusted and disappointed as she felt. "The same. She still won't say a word. Even when I grounded her from watching television for being rude, she didn't argue. She flounced to her room and stayed there all evening."

"Oh, Alex. I'm so sorry."

He rubbed his forehead as if the motion would smooth out his worry wrinkles. "I'm at my wits' end. I've talked until I'm hoarse, but she doesn't respond."

"I can't blame her for not wanting her life to change. She doesn't want to share you with anyone."

"Life is all about sharing. I obviously failed to teach her that important lesson."

"Don't be so hard on yourself. You did your best. As for Jennie, she's as smart as her father. She'll come around."

"She'd better," he warned darkly. "Or else."

"Or else what? You can't threaten her, Alex. She'll only resent me more than she already does."

"But she shouldn't resent you *at all.*" He began to pace.

After the good times she'd shared with Jennie, the youngster's rejection hurt more than she cared to admit. "No, she shouldn't, but give her time, Alex."

By Friday, however, Claire was surprised that Jennie's attitude hadn't softened. It required a lot of energy to fuel anger for several days, and Claire tried to think of a way to defuse the girl's rage. But how? If the youngster wouldn't talk to her father, then Claire's chances for success were far more slim.

It became even more obvious when Mrs Rowe dropped Jennie off at the clinic after school because she was leaving town to visit her daughter over the holiday. Claire saw her sitting in Alex's office and stopped to chat.

"Are you excited about your pageant tonight?"

Jennie pointedly looked in another direction. "I guess."

Claire ignored her hostility. "Someone brought home-made fudge today. If you'd like a sample, I'll bring a few pieces for you."

"I can help myself."

"Look, Jennie, I know you want all of your dad's attention, but don't you want him to be happy?"

"I make him happy."

"Yes, but four people can have twice as much fun together as two. And if you and your dad set aside a special time to be alone, I wouldn't object. Joshua and I'll do it, too."

"We don't need anyone else."

"Maybe you don't, but I do. I think your dad needs me, too."

"No, he doesn't. I won't let him," she said on a rising, frantic note.

Claire noticed the flash of fear in Jennie's eyes. "What are you afraid of?" she asked gently. "No matter what, he'll always love you."

Jennie glared at her. "I know that. But you were just supposed to be a friend."

"I still would be," Claire said softly.

Jennie clamped her mouth shut and didn't answer. She sat sullenly in the chair, swung her legs back and forth and crossed her arms.

Claire's hopes died. She didn't claim any expertise in child psychology, but Jennie was too stubborn for Claire to anticipate a simple answer or a speedy resolution to their problem.

She'd been effectively dumped on the horns of a dilemma. If she and Alex continued to see each other away from work, Jennie would make his home life miserable and eventually place him in the position of choosing between her and his daughter.

Or she could walk away and save everyone a lot of grief.

"This isn't going to work, Alex," she told him after they'd seen their last patient.

"It will. You'll see."

She shook her head. "I thought so, too, at first. But I talked to Jennie this afternoon."

"You did? What did she say?"

"Not much, but this is more than a case of jealousy over sharing you with someone else. Remember how she looked when you told her about us? She was horrified."

"Because she didn't want her life to change. You've already said that."

"Yes, but now I wonder... I think she's scared. Really and truly frightened."

"That's ridiculous. Why should she be afraid?"

"I don't know, but she is. Until we find out, I think it would be better if I stayed out of the picture." She paused. "I've wrestled with this all afternoon and decided it would be best if Joshua and I didn't attend Jennie's Christmas pageant this evening."

"No." He shook his head. "She wants to drive a wedge

between us and if you stay away, she'll think she's succeeded. I won't play into her hands.''

"What choice do you have? It won't be fun for anyone if being around me upsets her.''

"The point is, *I* want you there.''

"I've made up my mind.'' She paused, hating what had to come next but knowing she didn't have a choice. "You asked me to consider marrying you. Well, I have, and my answer is no.''

CHAPTER ELEVEN

"NO?" ALEX raised his voice. This definitely wasn't news he wanted to hear. *"No?"*

Claire didn't cower under his tone. "I'm sorry. I've thought it over these last few days. I won't marry you under these circumstances."

Her words weren't direct quotes of what his now ex-wife had said, but they were close enough. *I can't handle this, Alex.*

Nothing he'd said had been able to change Donna's mind and now it seemed to be happening again. The anger he'd felt then suddenly resurfaced and he lashed out.

"Maybe you can turn your love for someone on and off at will, but I can't."

"Oh, Alex," she said mournfully. "I haven't stopped loving you. I won't."

Music to his ears. His hurt faded.

"Loving you or not isn't the issue," she continued.

"You're going to let an eight-year-old affect the course of your life? To deprive you of what you want most?"

"This eight-year-old is going to affect the course of my life, one way or another," she explained.

"Jennie's mother ran away when things got tough. I didn't think you would, too," he accused heartlessly.

Claire bristled. "You're hitting below the belt, Alex. This has nothing to do with running away because things are tough. I want us to be together, too, but I can't fix Jennie's attitude as easily as the surgeons repaired her physical problems. I would if I could, but it isn't that simple.

"Believe it or not, she's going to set the tone of our

household. I refuse to come home every night to a battle-
field and watch her force you to choose sides. I won't
subject Joshua or any other children we might have to
those living conditions.''

He hadn't thought that far ahead, but filling the bed-
rooms in his large home with sons and daughters would
be a pleasure.

"It wouldn't be like that," he insisted. "I won't let it."

Her sad smile was more than he could bear. "There are
some things you can control, but Jennie's acceptance, the
way she feels about me, isn't one of them. You can't
ground her forever. Once she's older and has driving priv-
ileges, things could get so much worse. She could under-
mine me in your eyes, or cause so many problems that
they would eventually tear us apart. In the end, she'd
win.''

Claire was right. If Jennie's outlook didn't change, those
teenage years could be worse than a nightmare, but Alex
wasn't about to give up without a fight.

"Maybe if we both back off for now," she said softly,
"Jennie will think the threat is gone and she'll explain
what's going on inside her head.''

"She knows we'll still see each other every day, even
if we don't spend our evenings together.''

"I've thought about that, too.'' She chewed on her
lower lip. "Oncology is advertising for a nursing position.
I think I should apply for it.''

"No! I won't let you." To lose Claire so completely
was unthinkable.

She spoke as if he hadn't opposed her idea. "It wouldn't
be that bad. If circumstances change, we can be together
in the evenings. I'd only be a phone call away.''

"No." He remained adamant.

"You can't stop me," she said.

"They'll ask for a recommendation.''

Incredulity appeared on her face and puzzlement in her eyes. "You'd give me a bad reference?"

Could he? Yes. *Would* he? The anger stiffening his spine faded and his shoulders slumped with the weight of disappointment. "No," he said quietly. "I wouldn't."

She moved next to him, her scent teasing him, her touch painfully sweet. "Look at us. See what's happening? We're already fighting."

"Some things are worth fighting for. I happen to believe our future is one of them."

"I do, too, but until we know what the battle is about, we're spinning our wheels. You said yourself that we moved rather fast. I'm suggesting that we slow down for now and give us, and Jennie, a chance to come to terms with the situation."

Claire hadn't totally written off their future, which he found promising. "All right. How long?"

She lifted one shoulder in a dainty shrug. "However long it takes."

"If you think I'm waiting until Joshua leaves for college, you can think again."

"Well, how am I supposed to predict a time frame?" She sounded exasperated. "She's your daughter."

Truer words were never spoken. "You're right. She is. And that means I'm responsible for straightening out this mess." Alex turned away, determined to begin before another minute ticked by.

"Alex." Claire's fear and worry was obvious. "What are you going to do?"

"I don't know yet, but I'm taking control of my home." Jennie had ruled the proverbial roost for the past eight years and he'd allowed it. As he'd told Claire some time ago, the women he'd dated hadn't meant enough to him to shift the balance of power, but that had changed.

He grabbed his coat from the stand in his office, then strode down the hallway to find Jennie. From the smile on her face as she spoke with the ladies in the office, no one would have known how much havoc she'd wreaked in his life during the last forty-eight hours.

"Jennie, we're leaving. Now."

She blinked in surprise at her father's clipped tone, but he'd used it before so he knew she understood its implications.

He waited impatiently for her to slip on her coat while he said his goodbyes to the staff, then ushered her out to his vehicle in the parking lot.

She raced to keep up with his long strides. "Daddy..."

Alex was too frustrated by the women in his life to talk. If he spoke now, he would probably say something he'd later regret. He'd listened to her silence for the past two days—now it was her turn to listen to his.

"Do not say a word," he growled. "I'm not happy with you and you know it."

"But, Dad—"

"Not. One. Word."

She fell silent and crawled into the passenger seat, then he slammed the door and slid behind the wheel. He reached for the ignition, then stopped. "You have pouted and acted horribly rude to someone who's important to me. After the pageant, we *will* talk about this whole situation, you *will* explain your actions and there *will* be *no more* sulking or whining. And you're stopping this silent treatment as of right now."

He paused for breath. "Did I make myself clear?"

"Yes, sir," she said in a quiet voice.

"Good. Enough is enough."

The drive home passed in silence. "Grandma's here," she ventured softly as he rolled to a stop in the driveway.

"So I see."

Inside, he saw that defeat had replaced her previous animosity, but he hardened his heart against her sad expression. He'd come too far to back down now.

His mother greeted them both with a hug after she took their coats. "I pulled dinner out of the oven so you can eat a bite before you get ready for the pageant," she said cheerfully. "Why they schedule these things so early is beyond me. How do they expect people to have enough time to swallow their food when they work late?"

He bussed her cheek. "I don't know, Mom, but everyone seems to manage."

"All this hurrying isn't good for the digestion." She patted Jennie's shoulder. "Run along, dear. Your plate is already on the table."

Jennie cast an uncertain look in his direction, then obeyed.

"Bad day at the clinic?" Eleanor commiserated.

"A bad couple of days," he answered.

"Have a cup of my freshly brewed Earl Grey tea. You'll feel better."

He didn't want tea. He wanted coffee, the stronger the better, but since he knew his mother wouldn't have brewed a pot, he didn't argue.

Upon entering the kitchen, he found his mother chattering to Jennie about the pageant.

"I saw your costume," Eleanor told Jennie. "You're going to be the prettiest angel there. Claire did a beautiful job, didn't she?"

Jennie tentatively gazed at Alex. Curious how she'd respond, he raised one eyebrow at her. Her gaze fell to the floor as she mumbled, "I guess so."

"She'll be so pleased to see you wearing it tonight," Eleanor went on, plainly oblivious to the undercurrents in the room. "What time shall we pick up the two of them?"

Alex spoke over the mug in his hand. "We're not."

Jennie's eyes widened, but she didn't say a word.

"Oh, really, Alex. It's silly to take two cars when we can all fit in one. She'll have to juggle Joshua by herself and in this cold, too."

"She isn't coming." He looked at Jennie as she spoke, gratified to see his daughter look sheepish before she pushed peas around her plate.

"Oh, dear. She'll be so disappointed. Joshua isn't sick, is he?"

"No, Mom. He isn't sick."

"I don't understand."

Jennie jumped up. "May I be excused?"

Alex nodded and she fled from the room.

Eleanor cast a puzzled glance at the door Jennie had run through, then at Alex. "What's wrong with the poor child?"

"Long story, Mom." He gave her the condensed version, finishing with, "We *will* straighten this out. Tonight."

Eleanor nodded as she rose to refill her teacup. "Your plan could backfire."

That had been Claire's concern, too, but after a few days of politely tiptoeing around Jennie's sensibilities, it was time for action. "I'll risk it."

"On the other hand, Jennie has been the queen bee far longer than she should have been. You've spoilt her."

"Gee, thanks, Mom, for not telling me how you felt earlier."

Eleanor smiled at Alex's sarcasm. "If I had, would you have listened?"

Alex thought about it. Would he? Probably not, simply because he hadn't had a reason to do so.

"No matter how badly you want it, Jennie may never come around."

The thought was too scary to contemplate for longer than a second or two. "I know."

She slowly nodded before she cleared her throat and spoke briskly. "Yes, well, we're going to think positively. My granddaughter may be stubborn, but she isn't stupid." Her eyes narrowed behind her glasses. "You do realize that once you and Jennie straighten things out, you're not home free. Claire won't be easily convinced that Jennie's experienced a change of heart. She'll need a dose of strong convincing.''

"I know, but I can only go one step at a time, Mom. One step at a time."

The Thomas Jefferson Elementary School gymnasium was filled to capacity with parents, grandparents and siblings of the students. Alex ushered his mother to a seat, realizing how few of the parents around him had come alone. A good number were divorced, but mothers had brought stepfathers and fathers were accompanied by stepmothers, making him feel like an oddity.

He wanted Claire at his side, not a stranger. Yet if all went well, he wouldn't sit at the next Christmas pageant with only his mother for company.

The program was blissfully short—an hour—and later the only part he could recall with any clarity was the ten-minute segment when Jennie had stood on stage. Her costume was the most angelic, in his opinion, and he regretted not bringing his video camera. If Claire couldn't see the show in person, she might have enjoyed seeing the taped version.

"Thank you for coming," Mrs Kennison, the principal, announced as the last shepherd herded his "sheep" off stage. "We know how busy everyone is this close to Christmas, but we hope you'll stay long enough to enjoy the PTA's cookies and punch in the cafeteria. Have a wonderful holiday and we'll see you next year."

Alex didn't want cookies or punch, but the people flocked in that direction and he couldn't fight his way out of the pack. "Have you seen Jennie?" he asked Eleanor.

"No, but I'll watch for her," she replied.

Before he reached the refreshment line, he noticed Joyce Morris with a small group of people, appearing more re laxed than when he'd seen her in his office. She said something to her companions, then approached him.

"Hello, Alex. It's good to see you," she said.

"Same here. How's the arm?"

She tapped the cast through her sling. "It's fine. I want to thank you for everything the other day."

"I was glad to help. I assume you haven't had any problems with Rick?"

"No. If he wants to contact me, he can go through my attorney." She laughed. "I can't believe I feel like a new person. I should have left him ages ago."

"I'm glad to hear you're happy. I hope everything works out the way you want it." He glanced around the crowd. "Have you seen Jennie?"

Joyce pointed with her good hand. "She's standing over there, talking to Wendy. Those two girls have been thick as thieves the past few weeks."

A suspicion began to take root. "They have?"

"Oh, my. Talking on the phone for hours. When our life settles down, maybe she can spend the night."

"Yeah, sure. We'll work something out. Merry Christmas."

He strode toward Jennie and as soon as she saw him, he swore her face paled two shades. "It's time to go."

"I have to get my coat. It's in my classroom." She bid her friend goodbye, then hurried away.

On the way home, he listened to his mother's gushing praise of the pageant while he impatiently waited for his showdown.

"Goodnight, Jennie, dear," Eleanor said as she got out of Alex's car.

"'Night, Grandma."

"Hurry inside before you catch cold," she instructed.

"OK. Bye, Grandma." Jennie hurried to the porch, then called out, "Daddy, Grandma, come and see what someone brought!"

Alex frowned. "What in the world…?" He bounded up the steps and saw Jennie peering into a large trash sack. "What is it?"

"There are Christmas presents in here," she said excitedly. "I hope they're ours."

He didn't know who might have played Santa. "We'll check the tags, but let's go inside where it's warm," he said. The large box was heavier than he'd anticipated and he was equally surprised to recognize Claire's handwriting on the labels.

"They're from Claire," he said.

"How nice." Eleanor beamed. "What a wonderful surprise for both of you."

"Isn't it?" He glanced at Jennie, whose enthusiasm at receiving an unexpected gift had suddenly dimmed. "Put them under the tree and get ready for bed."

Jennie obeyed without argument.

As soon as he was alone with Eleanor, she laid a hand on his arm. "Be firm, but not too hard on her."

He nodded.

"And you'll let me know how your heart-to-heart turns out?"

"I will."

"I'll cross my fingers for a good report."

"Me, too, Mom. Me, too."

Claire watched the hours creep by, mentally picturing Alex's and Jennie's activities. At six-thirty, she imagined them arriving at the school. At seven, she saw him in a gym full of parents and heard the hush descend as the pageant began. At seven-thirty, Jennie walked on stage in her angel costume, the gold trim around her neck, sleeves and hem sparkling under the spotlight as she recited her rehearsed lines.

Joshua would have loved seeing the play, especially seeing his buddy, Jennie. Maybe next year, Claire consoled herself.

Next year, that was, if Alex with his "full steam ahead" philosophy didn't do more harm than good. She wanted him to succeed, but he couldn't dictate people's acceptance, not even his own daughter's.

She hoped Jennie would like the gift. If only she could stitch the rift in their relationship as easily as she'd stitched her costume.

Yet all wasn't lost. Even if things didn't work out, she still had Joshua and she'd regained Christmas. While she'd always remember that last season with Ray, she'd put the fierce sadness completely in the past. She had Alex and Jennie to thank for that.

Alex perched on the edge of Jennie's bed and studied his daughter. "What do you have to say for yourself, young lady?"

She immediately burst into tears and flew across the comforter into his arms. "I'm sorry, Daddy. I didn't mean to be nasty, but I wanted Claire to be a friend, not a step-mom."

"Why didn't you want her to be your stepmother?"

"I was scared."

He patted her back and remembered that Claire had suggested the same thing. "Why? What did Wendy tell you?"

She sat up. "How did you know about Wendy?"

"When I saw you two together, I guessed," he said. "So what did she say?"

"Wendy's mom told her that she needed a husband and Wendy needed a dad. Then, after they got married, she didn't have time for Wendy any more 'cause Mr Morris wanted all of her attention. He was mean to Wendy, too, and when she told me how he hurt her mom's arm, I was afraid the same thing would happen here."

No wonder she always stated that she didn't *need* a stepmother. "Oh, honey, everyone's situation doesn't turn out like Wendy's."

"Yes, it does," she insisted. "The other kids in my class told me how they hate their stepmoms and stepdads. They all wish they could go back to the way things were."

"Do you really think they're as unhappy as they claim? Callie gets along well with her stepfather and Joey likes his stepmother." He knew because they were his patients. Callie's father was a regular jail resident and Joey's mother was a chronic alcoholic. Both of their stepparents were doing a far better job than their "real" counterparts.

She shrugged.

"In some cases," he continued, "it's easy to look back and see the fantasy of the way it should have been instead of the way it was. As for Claire, you liked her, remember?"

"People are nice to the kids until they move in. My friends told me that, too. How their moms and dads don't love them like they did before."

"Oh, Jen. Just because I love Claire doesn't mean I'll love you any less."

"You say that now, but I don't want my house to be like Wendy's where everyone argues and fights. They're living with her grandma now. I don't want to move. I like my house and my room." She wiped her eyes with the sleeve of her blue nightgown.

"Now, listen to me," he said, pulling her onto his lap. "For one thing, Claire and I aren't going to be like Wendy's mother and stepdad."

"How do you know?"

"You'll have to take my word for it."

"But he *hurt* her."

"Yes, he did, and he'll have to answer for that. Are you worried that Claire will hurt me?"

"Of course not. You're bigger than she is."

"Then maybe she should worry about me hurting her."

Jennie frowned. "You wouldn't hurt her. You're too nice."

"Isn't Claire nice?"

"Yes, but..." She fell silent.

"Do you think I'd mistreat Joshua? I'm bigger than he is."

"No, Dad. You wouldn't. You're not like Mr Morris."

"How do you know?"

"I just do."

Alex nodded. "It's the same way I know that Claire wouldn't hurt you either. I trust her because I believe she'll be good to all of us."

"But I don't want to share you with anyone."

"You aren't the only one sharing," he pointed out. "Josh has to share Claire with us. It works both ways."

"Oh."

"I won't promise that we won't have arguments or that you won't have times when you're unhappy with Claire and Josh, but every family suffers through disagreements, even those where the parents stay together."

"Do you think so?"

"Of course I do. Grandma and I have gotten into a few lively discussions, but when it's all over, we still love each other."

"Do you love Claire better than my real mommy?"

"I loved your mother when I married her, but she chose to leave. Now I love Claire."

"More than me?"

"Someday you'll understand there are different ways to love people, but I love you both."

"She might not love me because of my scar and how I treated her."

"She doesn't care about your scar," he reassured her. "As for the way you treated her, I think she'd forgive you if you asked."

She nodded, looking thoughtful. "Maybe we should buy her a Christmas present. Josh, too."

He couldn't have been happier to hear her mention it. "Any suggestions?"

"Yeah, but it's sort of expensive. I'll even give you my piggy-bank money if you don't have enough."

Jennie's offer was a boon he hadn't expected, but it could prove to be the one thing that would convince Claire of Jennie's sincerity. He grinned as he tickled her tummy. "It's a deal."

Claire cleaned house all day on Christmas Eve and now that night had fallen, carols drifted out of her stereo as she dressed Joshua in his footed pajamas and played with him on the floor in front of their tree. Every now and then Joshua would point to the twinkling lights and exclaim "Pwetty" before he asked about Santa.

"Santa's coming tonight," she told him. "You can open your presents in the morning."

"Morning?"

"After we get up," she said, settling him on her lap in order to read the Christmas story to him.

The innkeeper had just said he had no more room at his inn when the doorbell rang.

"Bell," Joshua exclaimed as he clambered to his feet and ran to greet their visitor.

Wondering who would visit on Christmas Eve, Claire was very surprised to see Alex standing on her porch with a red Santa hat on his head. "Alex!" she exclaimed, feasting her eyes on him. "What are you doing here?"

"We've come to see if there are any good little boys and girls at this house."

Suddenly she noticed Jennie half-hidden behind him. She wore a perky elf hat, but her expression was far from perky. The youngster glanced at Claire, then looked down as she dug her hands in her pockets and the toe of her shoe into the floor. Her previous belligerence wasn't evident, but she obviously wasn't excited to be back at Claire's house.

The thrill of seeing Alex drained away as if someone had pulled the plug in her bathtub of happiness. He'd forced Jennie to come, plain and simple. Hadn't he realized that she, or any child for that matter, wouldn't respond to such heavy-handed tactics?

Be that as it may, she couldn't leave them on the porch. Yet as Alex waltzed in with a smile on his face, her blood began to simmer. After sitting at home, fretting and stewing while she cleaned her house until the spiders scurried away in terror, he had a nerve thinking that he could walk in and pretend everything was perfect.

"What *are* you doing here?" she asked, conscious of Jennie's awkward demeanor. "You should be at home, like everyone else, letting Jennie open her presents."

"Santa hasn't brought hers yet," he announced, dropping a large bag at his feet. "The only packages under our tree are the ones you gave us. We decided it would be more fun to open them with you. So here we are."

From the way Jennie averted her gaze, Claire suspected that Alex meant "I" instead of "we."

"Do you mind if we take off our coats?" he asked, already shrugging his off his shoulders.

"No." She took his, then Jennie's, feeling as if she'd lost complete control.

"Great. Come on, kids. Let's see what's in our bag."

Joshua and Jennie hurried into the living room, leaving Claire in stunned amazement. She quickly hung their coats in the closet before joining them.

"Alex," she warned, watching him crouch down in front of the Christmas tree and begin unloading brightly wrapped boxes from his Santa sack.

He acted as if she hadn't spoken. "Here's one for Joshua. Another for Joshua. One for Jennie. Claire, here's yours and…'' he pulled another from his bag ''…here's mine.''

''Alex,'' she said sharply, ''could I see you a minute? In the kitchen?''

He rose. ''Jennie, make sure Josh doesn't touch anything until we get back.''

In the kitchen, Claire turned on him. ''What is the deal?'' she hissed. ''You forced Jennie to come, didn't you?''

''Actually, I didn't.''

''Yeah, right. I have two eyes in my head and I can see just fine. She's miserable. You've ruined her Christmas and—''

''She's just shy.''

Shy? ''Your daughter doesn't have a shy bone in her body.''

He cupped the side of her face. ''Tonight she does. Trust me.''

Suddenly, Joshua's howl and Jennie's ''Dad, he's ripping the paper'' interrupted them. Alex kissed her swiftly. ''Relax. You worry too much.''

I worry too much? she fumed inside, but she couldn't argue because he was already gone.

Only because I have a good reason to worry, she mentally added. Alex hadn't shed any helpful light on the situation and now she was forced to crawl through a potential minefield.

''Are you coming, Claire?'' he called. ''The natives are restless.''

Succumbing to the inevitable, she squared her shoulders, pasted a smile on her face and re-entered their impromptu gathering.

''Claire, you get the sofa,'' Alex commanded as he wiped away the huge tear on Joshua's cheek before he placed him on the floor next to his small pile of packages.

Jennie sat next to her large box while he took his position near Claire's feet.

"Here's the plan," he said. "We're going to open them one at a time. Josh is the youngest, so he goes first."

He didn't need a second urging. The moment he grabbed hold of a package, he poked his finger into a seam and ripped. Jennie helped him take off the lid and he crowed with delight over his new toy trucks, puzzles and driving simulator.

"Jennie's next," Alex announced.

Claire watched her reaction with bated breath as the youngster opened her present. Her eyes widened and suddenly she burst into sobs.

Claire wanted to howl herself. Her idea of giving Jennie something that would cultivate a common interest had bombed. She looked helplessly at Alex and he simply shrugged, as if he, too, was at a loss.

"Oh, Jennie," Claire said after her sobs turned into hiccups, "if you don't like it, we can take it back. You can choose something else."

"I don't want to pick something else," Jennie wailed.

"Then what's wrong?" Claire asked, although she didn't expect Jennie to be any more forthcoming than she had been.

"I feel so bad." Jennie's breath came in gulps.

"Why?"

"For being nasty to you." She wiped her eyes with her fingers and sniffled. "I'm sorry for being crabby and mean."

Jennie's sincerity brought tears to Claire's eyes and she was speechless.

"Can you forgive me?" Jennie asked in a small voice.

Claire glanced at Alex and puzzled over his raised eyebrow. Now she understood why he hadn't seemed concerned when she'd pulled him into the kitchen. She'd assumed Jennie had been miserable when, in fact, she'd been shy and nervous, as Alex had said.

Overcome by the apology, Claire knelt beside Jennie and gave her a huge hug. "Thank you for apologizing. I appreciate it so very much."

"Can we be friends again?"

She wanted to be more than friends, but it was a start. "Of course."

Jennie wiped her eyes. "OK, Dad. It's your turn."

With the mood lightened, Claire protested, "If we're going by age, I'm after Jennie."

"True," Alex agreed, "but we're saving the best for last."

She couldn't argue with that, so she patiently watched him unwrap his present in short order. A pleased smile appeared as he slipped his new watch onto his wrist. "Just what I needed and exactly what I wanted. Now I'll always be on time. Thank you."

"Claire's next," Jennie informed them.

Jennie and Joshua climbed onto the sofa next to her. "Open," Joshua demanded.

Inside the shoebox-sized package, Claire found another wrapped box. "This is a trick gift, I see," she joked as she ripped through another layer, only to reveal another, smaller box. It reminded her of the Russian stacking dolls she'd bought her mother several years ago.

"You two must have used an entire roll of paper."

Alex grinned. "Not quite. Keep going. You're almost there."

The final layer of paper hid a small jeweler's box that was too small for a necklace or a bracelet. "Oh, my," she said, staring at it as if it might be a mirage.

"Go ahead. Open it," he urged.

She glanced at Jennie. The child's eyes sparkled as she nodded. "Daddy bought it, but I gave him my allowance to help him afford it. So it's from both of us."

Claire opened the velvet case and found a ring nestled inside. The large diamond was surrounded by smaller, colored stones. "How beautiful."

"It's a combination engagement and family ring," Jennie advised her importantly. "The little pieces are supposed to be all one color, but we thought it would be better if each one was our birthstone. I'm blue, Josh is green, you're pink and Daddy's red. The jeweler man said we can add more if we need to."

Claire struggled to speak. "I don't know what to say."

"Then I'll say it for you," Alex said as he took it from her and placed the ring on her finger. "Yes, Alex, I'll marry you and make a home with you and Jennie and Joshua."

Tears came to her eyes and she brushed them away. "I'm overwhelmed. I'd wanted this so badly and I was so afraid it wouldn't happen."

Alex rose to his knees beside her. "We know all about being afraid, don't we, Jen?"

Jennie nodded. "Yeah, but we're not afraid any more, so you shouldn't be either."

Claire eyed the diamond as it sparkled under the lamplight. "It's beautiful. And you really don't mind if I accept this?" she asked Jennie.

"No. I'm going to share my dad with you and Josh, and Josh has to share you with me and my dad."

Alex squeezed her hand. "You see? We worked everything out."

Claire glanced at Alex, aware of how close his mouth was to hers. "I never thought I'd ever be this happy again. I honestly was dreading tomorrow."

"You should never dread tomorrow," he said softly. "We never know what wonderful things it holds for us."

He was so very right and she told him so. "Thank you. For everything."

"The feeling is mutual." And he sealed their fate with a kiss that Claire would remember forever.

LIVE THE EMOTION

Modern Romance™
...seduction and
passion guaranteed

Tender Romance™
...love affairs that
last a lifetime

Medical Romance™
...medical drama
on the pulse

Historical Romance™
...rich, vivid and
passionate

Sensual Romance™
...sassy, sexy and
seductive

Blaze Romance™
...the temperature's
rising

27 new titles every month.

Live the emotion

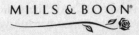

MILLS & BOON®

MB3

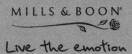

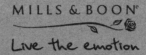

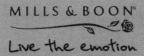

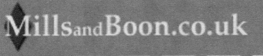

FREE

4 BOOKS
AND A SURPRISE GIFT!

We would like to take this opportunity to thank you for reading this Mills & Boon® book by offering you the chance to take FOUR more specially selected titles from the Medical Romance™ series absolutely FREE! We're also making this offer to introduce you to the benefits of the Reader Service™—

★ FREE home delivery   ★ FREE gifts and competitions
★ FREE monthly Newsletter   ★ Exclusive Reader Service discount
          ★ Books available before they're in the shops

Accepting these FREE books and gift places you under no obligation to buy; you may cancel at any time, even after receiving your free shipment. Simply complete your details below and return the entire page to the address below. *You don't even need a stamp!*

YES! Please send me 4 free Medical Romance books and a surprise gift. I understand that unless you hear from me, I will receive 6 superb new titles every month for just £2.60 each, postage and packing free. I am under no obligation to purchase any books and may cancel my subscription at any time. The free books and gift will be mine to keep in any case.

M3ZED

Ms/Mrs/Miss/Mr ....Initials ....
                                                                          BLOCK CAPITALS PLEASE

Surname ....

Address ....

....

....Postcode ....

Send this whole page to:
UK: FREEPOST CN81, Croydon, CR9 3WZ
EIRE: PO Box 4546, Kilcock, County Kildare (stamp required)

Offer valid in UK and Eire only and not available to current Reader Service subscribers to this series. We reserve the right to refuse an application and applicants must be aged 18 years or over. Only one application per household. Terms and prices subject to change without notice. Offer expires 31st March 2004. As a result of this application, you may receive offers from Harlequin Mills & Boon and other carefully selected companies. If you would prefer not to share in this opportunity please write to The Data Manager at the address above.

Mills & Boon® is a registered trademark owned by Harlequin Mills & Boon Limited.
Medical Romance™ is being used as a trademark.